"Do you mind answering one question, ma'am?"

Breathless for no good reason, Xan murmured, "No, of course not."

His gaze lowered to the black writing on the front of her T-shirt. It said, Bad Man Wanted!

There was nothing indecent in that stare, yet she felt her body break out in another wave of heat.

Judd Coltrain lifted his eyes. "What made you want to pick a Bad man for a husband?"

There was no way she could tell him the truth. He would be insulted to learn that after turning down Todd Bramforth's suspicious marriage proposal for the dozenth time, she'd blindfolded herself and had thrown a dart at her grandfather's map, announcing that wherever it landed, that was where she was going to go find herself a husband. So she told him another truth but one she felt he would accept.

"Where I come from, Bad men have a good reputation."

Dear Reader,

Harlequin Romance would like to welcome you back to the ranch again with our yearlong miniseries, **Hitched!** We've rounded up twelve of our most popular authors, and the result is a whole year of romance Western style: cool cowboys, rugged ranchers and, of course, the women who tame them.

So look out for books branded **Hitched!** in the coming months. We'll be featuring books by Val Daniels, Heather Allison and Susan Fox to name but a few!

Happy reading, partners!

The Editors,
Harlequin Romance

How the West was wooed!

The Badlands Bride
Rebecca Winters

Harlequin Books

TORONTO • NEW YORK • LONDON
AMSTERDAM • PARIS • SYDNEY • HAMBURG
STOCKHOLM • ATHENS • TOKYO • MILAN
MADRID • WARSAW • BUDAPEST • AUCKLAND

Dedicated to my darling new daughter-in-law, Lori, who
hails from the great state of South Dakota. Without her
help, and the help of her wonderful family, mainly
George, Janet, and Ervin, this book would not have
been possible.

ISBN 0-373-03409-1

THE BADLANDS BRIDE

First North American Publication 1996.

Copyright © 1996 by Rebecca Winters.

Printed in U.S.A.

CHAPTER ONE

BAD MAN WANTED FOR HUSBAND! Must meet the following criteria:

Must be single, must be a hard worker; must earn an honest living; must be debt free (truck or car loan and home or ranch mortgage acceptable); musn't swear, smoke, play cards or gamble; must be God-fearing, a temperate drinker and willing to attend church; must love children and want a family; must like to stay around home in free time and be a true companion; must be kind to all people and animals; must be fair; must be loyal and faithful; must have pleasant disposition; must possess a good sense of humor; must share every-thing with wife; must be tender, must look upon marriage as an equal partnership that will last forever.

If you are that man, and are in need of a wife with the same virtues, please bring this ad, along with a valid driver's license, a one-page résumé and a five-by-seven full-length color photograph to Wall's July 10 celebration.

Please present yourself between the hours of 10:00 a.m. and 10:00 p.m. to Ms. Xan (pro-nounced Zan) Harrington, 28 years old, 5'4", 120

*pounds, black hair, blue eyes, who will interview
you at the Bad Man Wanted Booth, Wall Rodeo
Grounds, Wall, South Dakota.*

Ignoring the crowds of curiosity seekers and disapproving women who'd been milling around her
booth all day long, Xan checked her watch for the
first time since taking a five-minute break over four
hours ago. It was almost ten o'clock and there were
still a dozen men to interview, even with the rodeo
in full progress and most everyone in attendance
for the calf scramble and businessmen's ribbon
roping.

After a sweltering day with a scorching sun, it
had started to cool off, but her body was still
radiating heat. She used the back of her forearm
to wipe the perspiration from her forehead and
urged the next man in line to sign his name to the
list, putting down his phone number.

So far, she'd gathered over two hundred names
and had promised each man that if she decided to
get to know him better, he'd receive a phone call
from her. At that point, he could ask *her* questions, and if he wasn't interested, he could withdraw
his name from the list.

However, if she didn't choose him, he wasn't to
take it personally since there were many factors involved. She promised to send him back his résumé
and photo with a small cash refund to cover the
cost of having the picture taken and of going to all
the trouble of coming to Wall to meet her.

Her forthright comments produced genuine
smiles and nods of approval from every candidate,

and all assured her they'd consider it an honor to get to know her better.

She'd purposely left off any physical description requirements. Men came in all colors, sizes and shapes. She'd been pursued by some of the most drop-dead handsome men in the world, and their physical attributes had meant nothing to her. At this point she had no preference in the looks department and figured she'd know the man she wanted to spend the rest of her life with when she met him and got better acquainted.

The problem was, she had no idea that when she paid for the ad, which had run every day for the last thirty days in the *Rapid City Journal* plus a few local newspapers in the western part of South Dakota, she'd get such a huge response. The men came from all parts of Pennington County and beyond.

Of course she expected a lot of men to show up whose only purpose would be to laugh at her, men who weren't the least bit interested in finding a wife. But what amazed her were the numbers of males from twenty-five to eighty who for the most part were polite, if a trifle on the quiet side, and seemed sincere and earnest in *their* quest for a wife.

They were so different from the men who'd been chasing after her since she'd turned sixteen—so far removed from the kind of men she wanted no part of—they could have come from a different planet. Which was exactly what she'd had in mind when she'd first contemplated finding a husband far from home, a man who didn't know she was an heiress, a man to meet her own exacting specifications, a man who felt *she'd been made for him, too*!

So far all the men who'd approached her booth with its red and white striped awning had come well-groomed and dressed up in clean or even new Levi's, plaid shirts and cowboy boots with a picture, résumé and license in hand, prepared to be considered as husband material.

Throughout the long, exhausting day, she'd separated the résumés into two stacks of what she thought of as possible or impossible candidates. The possibles were men whom she felt should be given a second chance.

The impossibles were basically men over forty-five, many of whom were widowers with large families. She couldn't see any of them wanting to start another family, even if they meant well.

The man she envisioned as her husband needed to have the energy to spend time with the children they would rear together. She didn't believe a hard-working rancher like these fine, upstanding South Dakota men had the time to be a dedicated father to two families.

Eventually, the last man wrote down his phone number, tipped his faded cowboy hat and left the booth. With a weary sigh, Xan reached for the pile of possibles and was shocked to discover that out of the two hundred plus applicants, there were only five résumés with pictures she'd put aside.

Hot color filled her cheeks when she remembered the rash statement she'd made to her house-keeper, May, the wonderful woman who'd raised her from the age of seven and had been like a mother to her. "Any Bad man would make a better husband than the men I'm used to associating with, May!"

Apparently that wasn't exactly true. Xan was much pickier than she'd realized. Slowly, she studied each of the five photos, but it was difficult to discern details when the only light available was coming from the rodeo stands where she could hear the roar and cheers from the crowd.

The one requirement she hadn't put in her ad was that there had to be a powerful chemistry between her and the man she chose as her husband. Over and over again she suppressed the niggling thought that not one of today's candidates had stirred her senses.

Xan could still hear May's last reminder as she got on the bus in New York to come to Wall. No matter how wonderful a man might be, without that certain chemistry between two people, a marriage couldn't and wouldn't work!

Convinced that May was speaking the truth, Xan was too hot and tired right now to know exactly what it was she was feeling. After a good night's sleep at her air-conditioned motel in Wall, she'd phone the five remaining candidates and on a second meeting, she'd probably discover that there was indeed chemistry between at least one of them and herself!

After all, each man had possessed a quality that had reminded her of May's deceased husband, John, an Iowa farmer who was a paragon in Xan's eyes and her ideal. When she found the man who could match *all* John's virtues, the virtues she'd listed in her advertisement, then she'd marry him!

As she bent over to put everything away in a plastic bag, she heard a deep male voice say, "I hope I'm not too late for an interview, ma'am, but I had to finish my chores before I could drive into town. The problem was, when I finally got my truck running, I didn't have time to make myself more presentable."

Xan stood up, shocked to discover that a man could look so disreputable and dirty yet appear so aggressively male despite his filthy overalls and suspenders worn over a dingy, torn, off-white T-shirt full of perspiration stains.

He had to be a foot taller than she was. Unlike some of the other men who wore a little too much after-shave in their effort to make a good impression, he smelled of horse and his own particular brand of sweat.

The four or five days' growth of dark beard and disheveled hair, which was almost as black as hers, gave him the appearance of a forty-year-old vagrant, the type of man she'd cross the street to avoid back home in New York City. Yet beneath the facial hair, she could see a forceful chin, rugged cheekbones and a straight nose, which would have been too prominent on a smaller man.

The lights were at his back, making it impossible for her to discern the color of his eyes shadowed by dark brows speckled with the dust from the road.

But even the obscure light couldn't hide the fact that he worked long, hot hours in the sun, which had turned the skin on his face and body to teak.

If she wanted proof of a man who put in an honest day's work, she had it in this strapping specimen whose hard-muscled arms looked strong enough to bend steel.

Wanting to be fair, she stammered, "N-no. You're not too late. I was just closing up. Did you bring a picture and a résumé?"

"No, ma'am. I don't have a camera and I'm saving every penny to pay off the loan on my ranch, which I won't own for at least ten more years. Of course, if there's a drought like there was this year, it could take longer."

In spite of everything, she felt a grudging respect for his stark honesty. There was no pretense here, no puffed-up pride.

"I don't need to have a picture."

"That's mighty kind of you, ma'am. You see, I didn't have time to make out a résumé because I only saw your ad this morning when my brothers drove down from Meadow to bring it to me.

"Of course, they checked you out first, and said you kind of looked like our mother used to look when she was young and the prettiest girl in the prairie states. That's when they brought me *this* and thought it would be worth my while to investigate, since I've been in the market for a good wife for a considerable while now."

His long, tanned fingers, callused on the underside, placed a copy of a small newspaper on the ledge of the booth. Apparently her ad had made the front page of a local paper called the *Bison Courier*, published every Thursday.

Dirt clung to the underside of his nails, but she had to remember it was dirt earned from working by the sweat of his brow. The only men she knew were Wall Street empire builders who worked hard at aggrandizing their families' fortunes by marrying women of similar backgrounds and fortunes to make sure all that money stayed in the proper hands.

"Since you've got your heart set on a Bad man, I figured I'd better get in to see you now. But if you'd said you were going to be at the Perkins County Fair in August, I would have had time to put a picture and résumé together and would have taken the trouble to get spruced up."

"Perkins County Fair?" she asked in a kind of daze, because the man had a way of talking that captivated her with his naturalness and lack of affectation.

"That's up in the northwestern part of the state where my brothers ranch. Every year there's a big to-do in Bison. You'd like it, ma'am. There's a flower arranging class, a 4-H fashion review, even a Calamity Jane show. Of course, there's livestock judging of the cattle and hogs. And right after that there's a queen contest."

He suddenly lowered his head and after a slight pause said in a husky tone, "My brothers told me that if you were to enter, you'd win, ma'am. After seeing you for myself, I dare say I have to agree with them. You've got eyes the color of larkspurs growing in the Slim Buttes when the morning mist makes them a real smoky purple, and you're even prettier than our mother. I didn't think that was possible.''

From the time she could toddle, Xan had been told she was a beautiful child. Since infancy, the adulation over her beauty had never stopped, particularly the continual reference to her jewel-like eyes framed by sooty black lashes men always compared to pure amethysts.

Those kinds of platitudes had never meant a thing to her because she felt that it was what was on the inside of a person that counted, not the face and figure God had given her, which she had done nothing to earn or deserve.

But she couldn't blow off this man's flattering remark. Comparing her to his mother put what he said in a whole other category, one that made her uncomfortable because she knew he had just paid her the supreme compliment. If she was honest, she had to admit she was touched....

He cleared his throat, as if he was embarrassed by what he'd said. His discomfiture made her warm to him even more.

"Lonnie, one of my brothers, has a camera and he could have taken my picture. As for my youngest brother, Ken, he learned to type in high school and he would have fixed me a fine résumé.'' There was another pause.

"I'm sorry to show up this way, smelling like a barnyard when you smell as sweet as a field full of ripe corn in a rain-filled wind.'' Once again Xan blinked at the unusual yet lovely compliment, which only a man who worked with the land might think to say.

"But I figured this was my only chance to meet you, and since this is what I look like most of the time, no fancy picture is going to change the facts. What you see now is what you'd be getting. Of course on weekends I'd clean up for you.''

To her consternation, Xan found herself wondering what he'd look like showered and shaved, dressed in a clean plaid shirt and Levi's. Her thoughts tumbled on as she tried to imagine him in chinos and a silk shirt, then wondered at her sanity for entertaining any thoughts of him at all. The problem was, she found herself charmed by his plain talk, which had a certain beauty, and there was something about his humility that prevented her from pitying him. "Look, Mr. . . .''

"Coltrain. Judd Coltrain. Pleased to meet you, ma'am.'' He held out a grubby hand. No telling what he'd been doing with it before he arrived at the rodeo grounds. After the slightest hesitation she placed her hand in his and he shook it like he would another man's. It was a strong handshake, straightforward.

No man of her acquaintance had ever greeted her this way before. His steady glance and frank, open friendliness underlined a rare, uncomplicated sincerity that caught her with her defenses down.

"My driver's license is somewhere in a stack of papers and magazines on the floor of my pickup.

But I was in such a hurry to get here before you left, I didn't bother to search for it.''

"That's all right, Mr. Coltrain. Just sign your name here and leave your phone number. As I told the other men, if I'm interested, I'll call you. If that should happen, naturally you might not be interested in me, and you'll have every right to tell me so without any embarrassment."

"That's fair," he offered in his low, vibrant voice, surprising her by not immediately asserting that he wanted to see her again. He was something of an enigma. After having to fight men off all of her life, his attitude presented a refreshing, if not confusing, change.

"The thing is, Mr. Coltrain—" she chose her words carefully "—if you don't hear from me again, please don't take offense. I'm trying to find the man I want to spend the rest of my life with, so I have to be very particular."

He nodded, as if what she'd said made perfect sense. "I feel the same way, ma'am. That's why I'm still not married. Appearances can be deceiving, especially ones like yours," he drawled, spelling it out without saying that a man might sell his soul for a woman who looked like her and regret it for the rest of his life. Everything about him either surprised or disarmed her.

"I reckon it's worth taking my time to find the right woman because I don't believe in divorce. My mother and father were married in our family church and stayed together forty-eight years before they both passed on. I aim to have a marriage like that. Otherwise, I'll just go my way alone.''

It was Xan's turn to nod because he'd taken the words right out of her mouth. ''I feel exactly the same way.'' May had worked for Xan's parents before they were both killed in a freak car accident when Xan was just seven, and May had assured Xan that theirs was a love match, just like her marriage to John. Xan wanted nothing less.

''There's just one problem, ma'am. I don't have a phone, so you'd have to contact me by mail.''

No phone? *Was he that poor?* It certainly sounded like it. Though millions of people lived without them, she had never known anyone personally who couldn't afford a phone.

''Then put your name and address on this list.''

''Be glad to.''

He took the pen she handed him. When their fingers touched, she felt a curious little shiver dart through her body. Without conscious thought, she found herself watching him to see what address he'd fill in, but she was threatened to be disappointed because all he put was his name in care of general delivery, Wall, South Dakota.

After he'd finished printing everything with painstaking thoroughness, much like a school-aged child, he looked up and stared hard at her. ''Do you mind answering one question, ma'am?''

Breathless for no good reason, she murmured, ''No, of course not.''

His gaze lowered to the black writing on the front of her pale pink cotton T-shirt, which she'd had made up at the famous Wall Drug when she'd first gotten off the bus in town. It said, 'Bad Man Wanted!'

There was nothing indecent in that stare, and nothing indecent about the shirt, which fell loosely over her full curves and was tucked in the waistband of her jeans, yet she felt her body break out in another wave of heat.

He lifted his eyes. "What made you want to pick a Bad man for a husband?"

To her horror, her cheeks turned crimson and she was thankful to be standing in the shadows. There was no way she could tell him the truth. He would be insulted to learn that after turning down Todd Bramforth's suspicious marriage proposal for the dozenth time, she'd blindfolded herself and had thrown a dart at her grandfather's map of the United States mounted on corkboard, announcing to May that wherever it landed, that was where she was going to go find herself a husband.

Appalled at the idea of anything so ludicrous, May told Xan to stop behaving like she'd lost her mind. But Xan was more determined than she'd ever been in her life. Though May mockingly pointed out that the dart had landed in the Bad River of South Dakota—which was no place to find anything, let alone a man—Xan didn't let that stop her.

She hurried over to the map and tussled playfully with May until the older woman got out of her way. It appeared that Wall, South Dakota, was the closest town to her dart, and she declared that

Wall would be her destination. After that, no amount of pleading on May's part would deter Xan from her goal.

But of course she couldn't tell Mr. Coltrain such an absurd story, even if it was the truth. So she told him another truth, a very recent one, in fact, but it was one she felt he would accept.

"Where I come from, Bad men have a good reputation." After meeting over two hundred Bad men in one day, her feelings toward them were very favorable.

Maybe it was a trick of light, but his eyes seemed to narrow as he studied her facial features, almost as if he could read her mind. "You're obviously not from around here," he observed wryly.

"No. I'm from the East."

"From the way you talk, I figured as much, but the East takes in a lot of territory."

His response was his subtle way of telling her he wanted to know more. But suddenly she wasn't all that eager to confide anything else to him. She had the oddest sensation that he was the one doing the interrogating, not the other way around, and it unnerved her.

"I'll tell you what," she said, clearing her throat. "Right now I'm in a hurry to get back to town. If I end up writing to you and you're amenable, then we'll meet at the Wall Drug for lunch and I'll give *you* a résumé."

He pondered her remarks, then said, "How long do you plan to be in Wall, ma'am?"

"I—I'm not sure."

"Well, if you're planning on leaving right away, that could present a problem for me—that is, if you decide you wanted to see me again. The fact is, I only come into town once every two weeks for my mail, which means I won't be back here again until the twenty-fourth."

Xan bit the underside of her lower lip. "I see." She found herself struggling for an answer because she really had no intention of contacting him again, yet she didn't want to hurt his feelings. "A-are you going back to your ranch tonight?"

"That kind of depends on you, ma'am. If you decided you wanted to get to know me a little better, I'd bunk down at the pastor's house on the edge of town and meet you tomorrow. He and his wife would let me freshen up. With their son and his wife and family living in Faith, they welcome the company when he's gone."

"You don't have to go to that kind of trouble on my account," she averred, wondering what she'd gotten herself into. It felt like she might already be in too deep to pull out gracefully without offending him.

"I'd like to, ma'am, if only to make my brothers feel better for thinking of me and trying to help me out in the wife department. It would be nice if I could tell them that you at least thought enough of me to share a meal with me. The thing is, I know a much better place to eat than the Wall Drug. It's quieter and they serve the best buffalo burgers you ever tasted. I prefer it to beef, myself, and eat it whenever one of my friends drops by with fresh meat.''

Xan's stomach rebelled at the thought, but she masked her features to show no reaction because he sounded so sincere and hopeful. ''I have to admit I've never eaten buffalo before and probably ought to try it while I'm here.''

''Then you'll meet me tomorrow?'' he asked in a low, quiet voice, almost as if he couldn't quite believe his ears.

''Yes,'' she murmured, not having the heart to disappoint him. After all, she'd come to Wall to find a husband. If she was too mean, too small, to refuse having a meal with one of the candidates, then she was the worst kind of hypocrite.

''Would eleven-thirty be all right? I need to hurry back to the ranch as soon as possible after that to get to my chores. I've got a field of hay to cut.''

''Of course,'' she answered, relieved to know he didn't expect anything more from her once they'd eaten.

''I'd pick you up in my truck but some of the springs in the seat are broken and it's not very comfortable. It might be best if you meet me at Pastor Swan's home. I'll write down his address, but you don't need to worry about getting lost. Everyone knows him. You can find his place on foot from any motel in town.''

''That will be fine.''

She noticed he was careful not to ask her where she was staying or how she was getting around. She liked the fact that he didn't pry into her personal affairs or attempt to get any friendlier.

"Ma'am, you've made me happier than a jackalope sunning himself on the prairie."

She frowned. "A jackalope? Don't you mean a jackaroo?"

"No, ma'am. Australian jackaroos are of the human variety. Jackalopes are native to South Dakota."

"I don't believe I've ever seen one."

"Well, now." He smiled for the first time, revealing a set of beautiful white teeth, which looked like they were all his own, and her heart lurched unexpectedly. "If I were ever lucky enough to have you step foot on my ranch, I'd show you one. They're elusive creatures, but I know where to find them."

She took a shallow breath. "Are they big?"

"Some of them."

"Are they dangerous?"

"That all depends."

"On what?" she asked, unconsciously putting a hand to her throat.

"I don't think ten-thirty at night is the time to discuss it. As my way of thanking you for having lunch with me tomorrow, let me take down your booth for you."

"Oh, no." She shook her head nervously, not wanting to prolong this meeting. "A Mr. Craven from town set it up and he said he'd dismantle it in the morning."

"Then I'll do it now and save Joe a trip."

"You know him?"

"Everyone knows Wall's oldest handyman. But after this celebration, he always has more work than he should take on, especially with his bad heart."

"I didn't realize."

"Of course not, because he never says anything. But his wife doesn't want him working any more."

She moistened her lips, which she assumed had gone dry from the heat and needed lipstick. "In that case, I'd appreciate your help." And she meant it. If Todd was here, he would never have given a thought to the booth or what would happen next, let alone offer to help out.

"I'll head for the truck and get some tools." Without waiting for her reply, he took off at a run and was back before she could countenance it.

Within seconds he'd untacked the sailcloth awning and with practiced ease had pulled the plywood apart, stacking it in a neat pile while she stood watching in stunned amazement at the speed and expertise of his movements.

"Did you buy all these materials including that stool you've been sitting on?" he asked when he'd finished.

"Yes."

"Where do you want me to put everything?"

"I was going to ask Mr. Craven if he wanted to keep any of those things. Otherwise I'll have to discard them."

He arched one dusty eyebrow. "If you don't mind, I can find a use for *all* of it."

He sounded deadly serious. A man as dirt poor as Mr. Coltrain had to be resourceful to make it in this monetary world, and she could only admire him for it. "I'm glad for you to take these things off my hands. It wouldn't seem right to waste the materials."

His head reared back, as if he was surprised by her comment. Or maybe she'd offended him in the way only a man with no money might be offended. She couldn't tell, but feared she'd said the wrong thing.

There was an uneasy silence, then, "I'll look for you at Pastor Swan's house at eleven-thirty tomorrow."

"I'll be there. Thank you for your help, Mr. Coltrain."

"Thank you for agreeing to have lunch with me. If you want to enjoy the full flavor of buffalo meat, don't eat breakfast before you come."

"I'll keep your advice in mind."

At this point, everyone was leaving the rodeo stands and the two of them were no longer alone on the grounds. Xan decided to melt into the crowd so he couldn't see where she'd parked her rental car. Something indefinable about him kept her on edge. All she wanted was to get back to the anonymity of her motel room and enjoy a long, cool shower and a hot meal.

Twenty minutes later, the phone was ringing off the hook as she let herself in the door of her motel room. Naturally it was May. She behaved like a mother hen with her newly hatched chick, overly protective and anxious. But Xan loved her dearly and had to admit it was good to hear her voice and discuss the day's events with her.

She flopped on the bed with a freezing can of Coke she'd purchased at a convenience store and began her tale, giving May a blow-by-blow account of her activities.

The older woman wanted to know which of the five finalists was the most interesting, a question that brought Mr. Coltrain's unforgettable image to mind.

Upset because the time spent with him had disturbed her concentration and fragmented her thoughts, Xan skirted May's probing question by explaining that she'd only *begun* her search for a husband. Give her another week to get to know the finalists better, maybe then she'd have some important news.

May didn't buy any of it. "Roxanne Harrington—" she always used Xan's legal name when she was upset "—face the facts. You don't feel any sparks, which means your experiment has been a miserable failure. Now I want you to get on the next available plane leaving Rapid City! Todd's out of his mind with worry and furious because I won't tell him where you are."

"I'm not in love with Todd," she announced with unswerving conviction, which must have rung true.

May responded in a quieter voice, "I believe you, lovey, but it's still time to come home."

Part of her wanted to do just that, but another part hated admitting defeat. When Xan had conceived this plan, she'd been so certain that she was doing the right thing, so certain that her destiny was tied up with a Bad man, she couldn't think beyond the moment.

Besides, she felt a curious sense of obligation to honor her commitment to Mr. Coltrain before she left the scene.

Oddly enough, she couldn't quite bring herself to mention him to May. There was no point, really. By two o'clock the next day, at the most, he would be on his way back to his ranch, out of sight, out of mind . . .

CHAPTER TWO

AFTER a restless sleep punctuated by a recurring nightmare of some faceless animal stalking her on an endless prairie with no human in sight, Xan woke up damp with perspiration, even though the air conditioner was doing its job.

According to the TV weather channel, the day would be a scorcher. By late afternoon the temperature would soar into the upper nineties with regional thunderstorms expected.

After showering and washing her hair, she opted for a sleeveless, white cotton blouse, modest khaki shorts and leather sandals.

With naturally curly hair framing her oval face, she didn't have to do anything more than run a brush through it. Other than a frosted pink lipstick and lotion, she didn't need makeup.

By eleven-fifteen she was ready to go and went outside the motel to start her car. The thought of buffalo burgers on an empty stomach made her slightly ill, but she was determined to be a good sport about it.

Mr. Coltrain had drawn a simple map, which a child could follow. Within a minute she'd turned onto the side street, which she followed to the edge of the small town. Even before she found the number of the tiny frame house she was looking for, she spied the tall rancher sitting on a porch swing with a white-haired gentleman who looked to be in his late eighties.

Mr. Coltrain must have recognized her immediately because he got to his feet and started down the steps. The pastor, not much taller than Xan, followed at a much slower pace.

Xan got out of the car, her gaze unconsciously taking in the rancher's surprisingly well-honed physique, which had only been a silhouette in the darkness the night before.

The same shirt and overalls he'd been wearing earlier were now free of dirt. Though shapeless and uninspiring, they couldn't hide his animal-like grace. Without hesitation he strode toward her in weather-worn cowboy boots, taking in the picture she made with one all-encompassing glance, robbing her of breath.

No dust caked his dark, well-shaped eyebrows today. He'd taken a shower, though he hadn't bothered to shave. Maybe he was growing out a beard and mustache. His hair appeared as untamed as ever and spilled over his bronzed forehead and onto the strong column of his neck.

Compelled by an urge she didn't understand, she sought his eyes whose color bordered on a translucent green with tiny gold and brown flecks in the outer portions of the iris. His gaze held hers until she grew flushed and out of sorts. Finally she glanced away.

"Ms. Harrington." This time when he extended his hand in greeting, she noted that his palms and nails were clean and that he smelled of soap. She couldn't help but be impressed that he'd gone to this kind of trouble to make himself presentable.

"So *you're* the Jezebel who's caused such a sensation in our part of the country," the pastor said with a broad smile and a wink, breaking her concentration.

Xan hadn't expected his remark to sting and felt the blood drain from her face. May had warned her that her experiment would cause most people to look upon her as a modern-day Jezebel. As far as Xan was concerned, May was a prophetess.

"Pastor Swan's just having a bit of fun at your expense, Ms. Harrington." The rancher came to her rescue in a rather gallant gesture for a man like him, surprising her with his sensitivity.

The older man shook her hand warmly. "Judd's right, of course. Pleased to meet you, young lady. Here he was fretting that you might not come over at all."

Again, Xan was surprised. Did he expect that she'd stand him up?

"I like your style. I like your ad and plan to use it in tomorrow's sermon. Seems to me if everyone was looking for the same thing in their partners that you are, there'd be peace on earth and love at home."

He gave the rancher a friendly pat on his broad shoulder. "Yes, sirree, Judd. You've found yourself a fine little woman in Ms. Harrington with all the qualities of your beloved mother, God bless her soul. I wish my Lydia was here to meet your prospective bride, but she went up to Faith a few days ago to be with the grandchildren and won't be back till Tuesday.''

Xan felt the rancher's probing gaze. ''Maybe that's just as well, Pastor. As Ms. Harrington and I discussed last night, lip service is one thing, living together forever quite another.'' This time a sensation not unlike a current of electricity charged her trembling body.

Xan was beginning to wish she hadn't started any of this.

''Amen to that.'' The pastor nodded. ''Now that you've met my Bad boy, here—'' he chuckled ''—you can forget the other candidates. Take it from me, they don't come any better or any finer than Amasa Judd Coltrain, and everyone in these parts knows it, especially the eligible females.''

Judging from the rancher's veiled eyes, the pastor had embarrassed *him*. Xan fought hard to suppress a smile hovering at the corners of her mouth.

''He's just been waiting longer than most for the right woman to come along.'' The older man kept right on talking, obviously crazy about Judd Coltrain and eager to matchmake. ''Of course when the word gets out that I've joined you two in holy matrimony, there'll be mass mourning for a while.

''But after you're married and start helping at the church socials and the like, you'll be accepted by the ladies. Just give them a little time to get over the fact that you were clever enough to steal Judd out from under their noses.''

This conversation was absurd, but Xan's lips curved upward anyway. She couldn't help it.

"Hold on, Pastor," Mr. Coltrain inserted. "You're way ahead of us. Ms. Harrington hasn't even seen where I live yet. That old adage about a man's home being his castle isn't exactly true, you know. It's the woman who stays put all day long, alone, and keeps everything running smooth."

A flicker darkened his green eyes, unsettling her, piquing her interest. "Ms. Harrington might not like my castle. She's from the East," he said solemnly, as if that explained everything. Strangely enough his comment irritated her because she had the distinct impression that he disliked Easterners, that there was something personal at the root of his antipathy.

"You don't have to worry, son. I've got her ad right here in my back pocket." Xan's blue eyes widened in disbelief as she watched him pull it out and peruse it. "I don't see anywhere on here that she's concerned about what kind of castle you provide for her. What she's saying is that she wants you to come home at night after an honest day's work, which is exactly where you should be."

The pastor paused to look at Xan and smile. "And if I had this lovely lady waiting for me by the hearth, I'd get my work done in a big hurry, you hear me, Judd?"

A bleak expression entered the rancher's eyes. "First she needs to get a good look at *my* hearth, Pastor.'

Apparently he was worried about Xan seeing his ranch house. Why did he act so upset? Did he think that she'd take one look at it and run away? The more she thought about it, the more she wondered if there'd been a woman in his past. A woman who'd rejected what he'd had to offer...

Since he didn't have much money and was forced to keep within a restricting budget, naturally he'd have little to show for it right now. Her grandfather may have left her a fortune, but when he first started out in life, she was confident he had less money than Mr. Coltrain. As for May and her husband, they struggled a lot during the first few years.

Did this rancher honestly think she'd ridicule him for his circumstances? Maybe it was because she was from the East that he'd formed such a negative opinion of her.

Or was he having second thoughts about a woman who would advertise for a husband in the newspaper?

"Why don't you take her out to your ranch right now and eat lunch on the way? I made plenty of food."

Startled, Xan said, "*You* put up a lunch for us?"

"I insisted on it." The pastor beamed. "Judd told me you've never eaten buffalo burgers before. That's my speciality when we have church barbecues. I wrapped them in foil so they'd stay good and hot for a while. I've also put in cold watermelon and some of Lydia's homemade bread.

There's honey, too, fresh from our beehives out back.''

"You're very kind," Xan murmured, not knowing what to say in the face of such generosity. She'd heard about South Dakota hospitality and could definitely vouch for it now.

"At first I thought you might like to eat on my front porch, but Judd says he's in a hurry to get his chores done before dark, so I put everything in a basket to be eaten on the way.''

Mr. Coltrain shook his head. "She won't like riding in my pickup, and I wouldn't let her drive her rental car on those dirt roads, Pastor. I think we'll just stay here and the three of us will enjoy the fine feast you've prepared for us.''

His comment made up Xan's mind for her.

"A-actually, I think the pastor's idea is a good one. I'd like to see a real working ranch, Mr. Coltrain. That's one of the reasons I'm out here, and I don't mind in the least riding in your truck. Naturally I'll help pay for the gas.''

His black scowl made her wish she'd kept quiet. "You'd better think twice on that, Ms. Harrington, gas money being the least of it. There's no air-conditioning in my pickup, and I won't be able to get you back to town before midnight, if then.'

Anger brought a tide of color to her face. "Do I look that fragile and helpless? I assure you, I'm not," she announced more crossly than she'd meant to, causing him to eye her for a long, uncomfortable moment, which could be taken several ways.

"Judd doesn't mean it," the pastor intervened kindly. "He's just squirming because he knows he's about ready to get hog-tied for good. I was the same way when I first met my Lydia. I knew she was trouble the second I laid eyes on her. You two go on from here and have a good time. I'll watch out for your car, Ms. Harrington."

"Thank you, Pastor. You've been wonderful."

"Say, you don't play the organ, do you?"

"No, but I can play the piano."

"Good. Judd's mother could play beautifully, too."

"I didn't say beautifully." Xan laughed because he was so impossible, and so nice.

"I guess we'll have to let Judd be the judge of that."

Did that mean he had a piano?

"My truck's round the back," Mr. Coltrain interjected in a no-nonsense tone. "While I get the basket, you might as well make yourself comfortable in the front seat, Ms. Harrington."

"I'll do that," she answered in a pleasant voice, ignoring his sarcasm. No matter what state his truck might be in, she refused to let him know it bothered her.

She shook hands with the pastor and started around the back of the house, her purse under one arm. A dilapidated Ford pickup, which had to be close to World War II vintage, stood in the drive, most of its paint rusted out so that she couldn't tell the original color. Maybe it was blue.

She climbed up on the running board and tried to open the passenger door, but it didn't work. Leaning inside the window, she noticed that the handle for it had broken off long ago, and that the window was down and would stay down permanently.

Five springs had poked their heads through the passenger seat, and there was so much junk mail and old magazines on the floor of the passenger side, her legs would probably stretch out in a horizontal position throughout the drive.

No wonder he hadn't been able to find his driver's license! Maybe he didn't even have one.

Not to be deterred, she walked around to the driver's side and got in, astounded that something that looked so ancient and dilapidated could still run.

She would never be able to stand those springs against her, so rummaging through the mess on the floor, she found a couple of dated Sears catalogues, which looked like they'd seen a century of use. They were at least four inches thick and would serve her nicely. She stacked them on top of the springs before she inched her way across and sort of slid onto them.

One thing about it, she was propped so high that for once she would be on eye level with Mr. Coltrain. Minutes later he found her that way, calmly waiting for him with a smile on her flushed face.

"Here," she said, reaching across the seat to take the black straw basket and settle it between them.

With seeming reluctance, he slid behind the wheel and slammed the door shut, whether out of anger or necessity, she'd never know. But it brought her up short.

"Look, Mr. Coltrain—" She played with the hem of her shorts. "It's obvious you don't want me to go out to your ranch, so I won't. I just didn't want to discuss it in front of the pastor. He's a darling man and I wouldn't like to offend him after all the trouble he's gone to."

His tanned hands stilled on the wheel. "What you're really trying to say is that you've changed your mind about spending the day with *me*."

She couldn't tell if he was hurt or not. "No. As a matter of fact, I'd very much like to spend the rest of the day with you. But I suddenly remembered how selfish I'm being, how much this is going to put you out. Last night you told me that you wouldn't be coming to town for two more weeks. I hate complicating your work schedule by forcing you to bring me all the way back to Wall tonight."

"Except for the fact that it's mostly dirt road after we leave Interstate 90, we'll only travel a hundred and forty miles, which is no great distance."

"Yet every time you take this truck anywhere, you put more wear and tear on it. Like you indicated earlier, you're trying to save your money. But you're also very kind because that's the way you're made. It's one of your most outstanding qualities."

36   THE BADLANDS BRIDE

She heard his sharp intake of breath and supposed she'd embarrassed him again, but she didn't care. It had to be said.

"The problem is, you're the first rancher I've ever known in my life, and from the little I've gleaned, you have an agenda that doesn't leave you time for unexpected visitors. It won't offend me if you want to take off now and eat your lunch en route. I'll walk around the town, grab a bite to eat and come over here later this evening for my car so the pastor won't think anything about it."

"Seems to me you're trying to get out of eating buffalo meat and are more worried about the pastor's feelings than you are mine."

"That's not true!" The interior of the cab rang with her spontaneous denial.

After a brief pause, he said, "Then prove it and come with me." His deep, husky voice resonated through her being. "My ranch is near the north rim in the Buffalo Gap National Grasslands. I have this hankering to show you your first jackalope. They come out right before a storm, and there's going to be a real beaut over the Badlands later on in the day, though you can't tell it now. Have you seen them yet?"

She shook her head, aware of a certain palpable tension between them that made her feel slightly light-headed and far too aware of him. "N-no. Only in pictures. I haven't had time to do any sightseeing." She'd been too consumed with finding herself a husband. "Why are they called that?"

"Because they look like a part of Hell with the fires burned out." When she darted him a shocked glance, a corner of his mouth turned up lazily and her heart gave another one of those funny little kicks, a reaction that seemed to be occurring with regular frequency in his presence.

"Those are General George A. Custer's words, not mine, ma'am. The Dakota Indians saw the erosion and called the area *mako sica*. Bad land. After a heavy rain, I like to take time off from my ranch to hunt for fossils. I've already found a three-toed horse and a small camel."

His piercing glance captured hers. "I've always had my heart set on honeymooning with my wife in those cliffs and spires and finding ourselves a saber-toothed tiger."

There was nothing conventional about this rancher! Here was a man who would want his bride all to himself where the two of them could get in touch with nature on its most elemental and primitive level. Forget the rest of the world.

What would it be like to be loved like that? Only for yourself, nothing else!

For a moment, Xan didn't say anything because his comment had captivated her. He was so different from Todd, whose idea of a honeymoon was to sail the Greek Islands on his family's new yacht, drink expensive French champagne and entertain important people on board.

Todd needed people. He said he needed *her*. But because of an accident of birth, she'd been born into a family destined to have more money than was humanly decent, and she'd never really know what had motivated Todd's marriage proposal, let alone the dozens of proposals from other men who'd been acquaintances of her grandfather.

Once more her thoughts shifted to the man beside her. With Mr. Coltrain, a woman would know exactly where she stood, and why. As far as she could tell, he didn't need anybody or anything. She sensed that if he took a wife, it would be because his deepest emotions were involved.

His love would be the forever kind.

Her heart ached for a love like that. That's why she'd come to Bad country. But she never expected to meet a man like Judd Coltrain. Could there be another male on the face of the planet anything like him? He fit no mold, no picture of her image of a husband.

She honestly didn't know what to make of him. If May asked her for a description, Xan wouldn't know where to begin. Nothing made sense, least of all how his unusual way of speaking and thinking tugged at her emotions.

Perhaps she ought to take May's advice and back out right now, before things went any further. She'd started this whole mess with that advertisement. Now the local pastor had become involved, and she and this virtual stranger were about to drive off alone somewhere.

And not just anywhere, Xan Harrington. He's about to show you his home, to let you look it over. You're crazy if you go. It's all crazy!

"Ma'am? I didn't mean to frighten you. If you've changed your mind about going with me, just say so. I wouldn't blame you for wanting to stay put. No doubt you've heard about poisonous prairie rattlesnakes and the grasshoppers, which are real bad right now. I won't lie to you about that. They've been attacking my oat and corn crops. Some say this plague matches the one back in thirty-five, which wiped out whole sections of the state."

"How terrible for you," she said in a shaken voice. Here she was, worried about unimportant matters when he was talking about his *livelihood* being threatened! If he lost all his crops, what would he do? How would he be able to keep paying on his loan?

To think that with one phone call placed to her banker in New York, she could have his entire balance paid off within minutes! *It wasn't fair.*

"O-of course I haven't changed my mind."

He was quiet so long, she thought maybe he hadn't heard her. Out of the corner of her eye, she saw his hand slowly drop from the steering wheel to the keys. Before he turned on the ignition, he eyed her broodingly. "You're sure about that?"

The unfamiliar gruffness in his voice alerted her that he was only trying to protect her, warn her. In his own way, he was very sweet, always trying to be tender with her. His sensitivity struck a deep chord.

"Yes," she assured him warmly. "But would you like to eat here first, or shall I feed you after we get out on the highway?"

"If you can manage it, I'd like to get started now."

"Then let's be off so you don't waste any more time. It's my fault you had to leave your ranch in the first place."

Again, his enigmatic gaze wandered over her, filling her with a mixture of excitement and trepidation, which she didn't understand. Just before he revved the engine he said, "How do you figure that, Ms. Harrington?"

She tried to ignore the mysterious chill that raced up and down her spine and averted her eyes, feeling inexplicably shy all of a sudden. "If I hadn't run that ad in the newspaper, your brothers wouldn't have bothered you with it, provoking you to come to the rodeo grounds to meet me."

"I don't recall complaining about it, but if you're accompanying me out of a sense of responsibility and nothing else, then I'd just as soon we said goodbye right now."

She fidgeted with the straps of her purse. Here was her chance to back out gracefully. But strangely enough, she found herself loath to part company with him yet. If she was being completely honest, she wanted to spend the rest of the day and evening with him. He fascinated and intrigued her more than any human she'd ever known, and he deserved the truth. At least as much as she was willing to share at this point.

"I—I ran a legitimate ad for a husband. Out of the two hundred plus responses, I only kept five sets of résumés and pictures of the men whom I'd like to get to know better. If you'd turned in a résumé and photo, that would have brought the total to six. Does that answer your question?''

''That depends on my competition,'' he replied unexpectedly. For someone with a slow drawl, his mind worked awfully fast. *Too* fast.

''I have no idea yet. Last night I was too tired to think about anything but a good night's sleep. I don't recall their names or faces.''

A long silence stretched between them as he put the truck in gear and backed out of the driveway, waving to the pastor, who waved back from the front porch.

Once they were on their way toward the road leading to the freeway, Mr. Coltrain murmured, ''Then none of the five made an impression worth a buffalo's hide, which means, *I'm* it.''

He said it matter-of-factly, neither disparagingly or gloatingly, and gunned the accelerator.

Xan would have liked to refute him, but her physical presence in his truck would have made a mockery of her words, and *he* knew it!

CHAPTER THREE

THE heat radiating off the pavement felt like an oven. Five miles out of Wall, Xan was dripping wet and panting with thirst.

Because they couldn't roll up their windows, insects of every size and description were swept inside the cab along with hot gusts of air that scorched her lungs. When she wasn't busy shooing them away, she quickly reached in the basket and found a couple of root beers, which the pastor had thoughtfully packed with their lunch.

Mr. Coltrain took a can and finished off his second burger. Though she dreaded tasting buffalo meat, it smelled exactly like hamburger, making her mouth water for food.

Eventually he turned his head, taking in the messy sight she made as she devoured some watermelon chunks, which were so ripe, the juice dripped down her softly rounded chin.

To her shock, he reached out with his right hand and caught a drop with his finger before putting it to his mouth. "Umm, that's sweet. I think I'll have some," he murmured.

Trembling from the brief touch of his skin against hers, she handed him the half-full carton and let him finish off the rest.

"You still haven't touched your burger," he commented in that low voice she felt resonate to every nerve ending in her body. "That's all right with me. If you lie to the pastor about how delicious it was, I'll never tell."

Sucking in her breath, she pulled a foil-wrapped burger from the basket and said, "I don't intend to lie."

"I'm glad to hear it. The thing is, once we get to my ranch, buffalo meat is all I have to offer, so if you don't like it and then get hungry later on, I'm afraid I won't be able to satisfy you."

She couldn't help smiling at the warning. "You sound just like May."

"May who?" prompted the deep voice.

"May Latta, my grandfather's housekeeper, the woman who raised me after my parents died. She's been like a mother to me, and she used to say the same thing, in the same nice way you just did. Better eat your beans and potatoes, lovey, because if you get hungry later on, there won't be anything else to satisfy you and I just hate to see you unhappy."

On that note she lifted the medium-rare burger to her mouth and took a bite, not knowing what to expect—just expecting the worst.

To her amazement, she discovered that buffalo burger wasn't that different from hamburger, or maybe it was the relish the pastor had put on the bun. Whatever, the meat had a richer taste than ground beef, and there was no fat. Within minutes, she'd consumed the whole thing.

All along she'd been aware of his probing gaze, which she finally turned to meet. "I had no idea buffalo burger was that good."

She expected her comment would please him. Instead, it seemed to produce an odd gleam in those shadowy green depths that took the sunshine right out of her day. *Didn't he believe her?*

Crushing the foil in her palm she asked, "Did I say something wrong?"

"No, ma'am. So far you're saying everything just right," he replied, sounding his affable self, but somehow she wasn't reassured. *What did he mean, exactly?*

Maybe he was still hungry. According to May, a man was easier to reason with on a full stomach. May had always used that tactic with Xan's grandfather—a difficult personality at best, an irascible man driven to make money.

After Xan's sweet grandmother had died of a bad heart, he'd traveled the country repeatedly from one end to the other doing business and hardly ever came home to see his granddaughter. When he did make the rare appearance, May and Xan did everything in their power to keep from getting in his way or upsetting him. "Would you like some bread and honey?"

"Why don't we save it until we get to the ranch. I'm going to be pulling onto a dirt road any second now, and the honey will act like a homing device to whatever's flying out there."

She quailed at the thought and immediately proceeded to clean things up and put them away in the basket.

True to his word, they exited the highway and followed a frontage road for about a mile. Then they turned onto a dirt road she hadn't noticed from the freeway.

It disappeared into a world full of long, wafting prairie grass, which met a hazy blue sky and unfolded in all directions, farther than the eye could see. To her right, in the far distance, enormous white clouds with sheared-off bands of gray forming the base had started to gather.

Perhaps Mr. Coltrain could sense her wonder at such a magnificent sight because he pulled to a stop, though the engine was still running, and let her drink her fill.

For the longest time Xan didn't say anything as she absorbed the stillness and lack of civilization and just let her imagination drift back to the era of the great Dakota Indian Nation. The buffalo they hunted might have thundered across the very terrain where the truck stood.

"It's incredible," she whispered and turned awestruck eyes in his direction.

Again she felt unaccountably disturbed because he said nothing and only continued to stare at her as if searching for something still eluding him.

"Visitors often get sick looking into so much open space." He finally condescended to speak.

Now she understood what was on his mind, and she nodded. "Yes, I've heard of that. Something like the opposite of claustrophobia. I once had a friend who said she got sick being surrounded by mountains. She always felt they'd fall in on her. Strange, isn't it? I suppose it has something to do with where you're born.''

''Where were you born, Ms. Harrington?'' He fired the question so fast, she didn't have time to think up a lie even if she'd wanted to.

''Topeka, Kansas.''

''That's not exactly the *East*,'' he ground out.

''No.''

Since he had every right to ask her questions, she decided now was the time to answer them.

''My parents died when I was seven. Apparently my dad and his father were estranged because I never saw my grandparents until they took me to live with them in New York City. Grandma died soon after, and I was so unhappy, I asked my grandfather if May could live with us. She'd come to work for my parents after her husband had been killed by lightning in his cornfield, and I loved her.

''Since Grandfather never wanted to stay home after Grandma was gone, he sent for May to come and take care of me. We've been together ever since. Grandfather died a year ago, so now there's just the two of us.''

After an uneasy silence, she cleared her throat. ''I envy you having brothers, but I'm not complaining, because I have May and she has taken the place of a whole family.''

"Except for a husband." The low aside sent a wave of heat over her skin that had nothing to do with the temperature outside.

"Yes," she whispered, glad he knew everything. Except that he didn't know she'd been left a fabulous fortune, which was a terrible burden.

May had to keep reminding her that the business her grandfather had built up over a lifetime had kept her alive and had given jobs to hundreds of thousands of people.

Xan could see May's reasoning, of course, and she agreed with it. But her grandfather had no philanthropic bent, and all Xan could think about were the many ways she wanted to put all the excess profit to better use.

The vast sums of money at her disposal were already making a real difference in the lives of people who had no resources and were forced to look to charity or foundations for help.

Todd had never said the actual words, but she knew he thought she was crazy to give so much away instead of reinvesting it. Though his family had money, it wasn't on her grandfather's scale. She had the awful suspicion that Todd was being the ardent pursuer because he couldn't wait to manage her finances, and he'd have to be her husband to do that.

It was a terrible thought, and if it wasn't true, then she was doing him a great injustice. But she simply didn't trust him or any other man she knew not to be influenced by the heritage left her.

The Royal Family in England couldn't help that they were born to a title, even if some of them didn't like it. Neither could she help that she was born a Harrington. And she couldn't help that she was different from her grandfather.

It made her happy to give up that money. After all, she hadn't personally earned it. It didn't belong to her by some divine right. It didn't make her better than anyone else.

For the first time in her life, she didn't feel a complete fraud. With May's down-to-earth advice, she'd been able to come up with new and innovative ways to help others who were incapable of helping themselves *without* diminishing the company her grandfather had created.

This brought her a certain amount of contentment. But as Mr. Coltrain had just reminded her, there was still an important ingredient missing in her life.

A husband probably was *the* most important ingredient. She didn't know because she'd never had one. Which was why she was out here on the grasslands with a prospective candidate right now.

"Are you ready to go on, ma'am?"

Xan no longer took offense at his pointed questions because they were simply his way of showing concern for her welfare. The truth was, she was growing to like him a lot more than she dared admit. He made her feel protected and cherished. So far, he seemed to possess many of the traits listed in her advertisement for a Bad man.

She didn't quite know what made her turn her head and ask, "Perhaps more to the point...are you? Remember—you have the right to back out at any time."

If she wasn't mistaken, his features seemed to harden for an instant. Now that he'd learned she was from New York, she had the distinct impression he was trying to frighten her off, probably because he feared she was too sophisticated to appreciate the hard life of a rancher, or to tolerate the isolation.

But if that was the case, she wouldn't have ventured west of the Mississippi, let alone to the heart of South Dakota where there were only nine people per square mile!

"If my brothers had been wrong about you, I would have gotten right back in my truck and headed for home." *And he meant it.*

For once in her life she was thankful she had the kind of looks that had drawn him to her. Otherwise they would never have met!

Curious how just thinking about that possible near miss produced a sense of loss that was rather staggering in its implication, considering she'd only known him since ten o'clock last night!

As if they'd wasted too much time already, he put the truck in gear and they took off over the dirt track. Xan bounced around like a storm-tossed ship riding a sea of rolling green waves.

While she tried to brace herself with one arm on the back of the seat and the other against the door frame, something started spattering the windshield. At first she thought it had to be hail, but soon realized her error.

"Dear God. They're grasshoppers! Thousands of them!" she cried in an unsteady voice. Despite the truck's speed, they came inside the cab with the hot hair and crawled on everything exposed, including her arms and legs.

"They won't hurt you," he muttered and turned on the windshield wipers.

She wanted to scream her lungs out, but suppressed the urge because Mr. Coltrain didn't appear to be affected by them and because she'd just told him she was ready for the drive. It would be humiliating to break down and beg him to take her back to town before they'd even gone a mile.

Using one hand to hold on so she wouldn't slide off the Sears catalogues, she brushed the disgusting creatures away with the other. But no matter how many times she got rid of them, more came back.

Ten minutes later she could smell something burning and flashed him an anxious glance. If the truck broke down in the middle of this nightmare, she knew she'd never be able to handle it. Swallowing hard she asked, "What do you think's wrong?"

"Nothing's wrong, Ms. Harrington," he said in a mild-mannered voice without taking his eyes off the road. "The grasshoppers like to crawl up underneath the hood. As soon as they land on the engine or cling to the fan belt, they start to cook. Whenever you smell that smell, you know you're almost home."

"H-how far is it?"

"About thirty more minutes."

The grasshoppers seemed to love her hair. She had to comb through the glistening black curls with her fingers to get rid of them. Copying Mr. Coltrain, she grasped them in her palms and threw them out the window.

While the truck penetrated deeper and deeper into the prairie, they worked in unison to keep the insects at bay, exactly like two shipwrecked sailors bailing water from a leaky lifeboat.

"To think the early settlers had to deal with all this on a twenty-four-hour basis," she exclaimed, hoping that a little conversation might get her mind off the situation and control her panic. "No roads, no trucks. What incredible people they had to be."

For a breathless moment she sensed his eyes on her, but when she looked over at him, he was staring straight ahead once more. In profile his hard, chiseled features—which the beginnings of a beard and mustache couldn't hide—reminded her that here was a pretty incredible man who would probably have been right at home on the prairie a hundred and fifty years ago without any problem.

When they arrived at his ranch house, she knew that before the day was out, he'd have to leave her long enough to cut a field of hay. There'd be more grasshoppers to face and more scorching heat. But it was obvious he didn't mind the adversity.

Rather, he appeared to thrive on it, which set him apart from the men she knew who sat in luxurious leather chairs in their air-conditioned offices and moved paper around, probably making more money in one day than Mr. Coltrain made in a year of backbreaking toil and labor.

She couldn't imagine Todd out here, working the land from dawn to dusk, putting up with droughts and bug infestations. Until now she had no conception of what it meant, and experienced a new wave of compassion for all farmers and ranchers. As far as she was concerned, they formed the backbone of America and she felt proud to be in Mr. Coltrain's company.

Afraid he would catch her staring, she looked out her window, brushing away more grasshoppers. The burned smell was worse than ever.

Eventually she caught sight of a lone structure out on the prairie, the only visible sign of civilization she'd seen since they'd left the highway. Though they were still a good mile away, she could tell it was tiny.

"Is that some kind of a storage shed?"

After a perceptible pause he said, "That's my house and the beginnings of my ranch, Ms. Harrington."

Horrified to have made such a blunder, she could have cut her tongue out, but it was too late for apologies.

She craned her neck to take in the details, then received the second shock of the day to discover he lived in a sod house.

Blinking, she cried, *"It looks just like a Laura Ingalls Wilder drawing, the kind of home she first lived in when they came to the prairie!"*

Forgetting her discomfort, Xan turned a hot, dusty, radiant face to Mr. Coltrain. "When I was young, I read her books over and over and over again. You can't imagine how much I loved them. I used to wonder what it would be like to grow up in her time. I always wished I could be Laura. I can't believe you live here!"

He muttered something unintelligible under his breath and brought the truck to an abrupt halt not ten feet from the house, dislodging some of the grasshoppers. Apparently he'd reached the end of his tolerance for the annoying creatures, but for once she was too excited to care about them and shook her head incredulously.

"Why didn't you tell me? I feel like one of my childhood dreams has just come true!"

He shot her an unfathomable glance before her rapturous gaze returned to examine the lines of the thick strips of sod piled like bricks to form the walls and roof with its bent smokestack.

She breathed in deeply. *No electricity, no telephone, no foreign cars, no showplace. Only the sky and the prairie.*

"It's perfect. I—I feel like I've traveled back in time and Charles Ingalls is going to come walking outside any second now."

Because Mr. Coltrain had jumped from his truck and had removed the picnic basket, she assumed he hadn't heard her. But as she slid across the seat to get down he said, "Sorry to disappoint you, ma'am, but I'm afraid you're stuck with *me*."

Then his strong hands were biting into her waist and he lifted her from the truck. Grasping his shoulders to stay balanced, she wasn't prepared for the feel of his rock-hard chest against her softness, the exquisite sensation of her thighs sliding down over his as he lowered her to the calf-high grass.

She'd been held and kissed by several men, Todd most recently, but she'd never experienced anything as remotely sensual as this. When he let her go, she was trembling so hard she lost her balance and fell into the grass.

He would have helped her up, but she scrambled out of reach and rose to her feet on her own, afraid for him to get that close again because of the way her body had responded to the feel of his.

He might as well have set the prairie on fire!

He should never have touched her. Now it would be all she could think about, dream about. He already seemed bigger than life to her, but she never imagined her body could come so achingly alive.

At last she understood what May meant about chemistry, the kind of fireworks that had to be there for two people to make a marriage work. Mr. Coltrain had experienced that mysterious alchemy, too, because what had happened between them just now was no accident!

He'd *wanted* to feel her close to him, otherwise he would only have taken her hand so she could jump down from the truck on her own.

"If you'll wait a moment, Ms. Harrington, I'll go in and turn on a lantern or two so you'll be able to see."

Nothing in his voice indicated that he was as disturbed by their encounter as she was, but she knew differently and nodded, incapable of saying anything while her emotions were in so much upheaval.

He took the stool and awning from the back of his truck. After shaking out the grasshoppers, he picked up everything, including the picnic basket sitting on the grass, and disappeared inside.

Maybe the little sod dwelling was going to be her home.

Xan's breath caught on the realization that this Bad man was the one she wanted for her husband. She didn't need weeks or months to make her decision. She knew it deep down inside the very core of her, just as surely as she'd known that her destiny was tied up with a Bad man.

The moment the hot, dirty, disheveled rancher had appeared at her booth and had started talking to her, she'd felt something burst into life that had been lying dormant all these years.

Like he said himself, if he hadn't found her equally appealing last night, he would have gotten in his truck and driven off without her ever having known he'd come to the rodeo grounds for a look.

She couldn't help but smile when she thought of his brothers, who'd taken the time to drive from another part of the state to see what she looked like. It meant that before going to his ranch, they'd had to travel all the way to Wall *first* for a good look at her. They'd had to make sure the interview would be worth his time.

In all honesty, she couldn't wait to meet them. If they hadn't been looking out for their brother, Mr. Coltrain would never have seen her ad in the *Bison Courier*, let alone any newspaper. He was too busy trying to keep his ranch going.

One thought led to another. If she married him, she'd have two brothers, whom she already liked because they loved their brother and wanted him to be happy. She couldn't help but be thrilled and flattered that with one glance, they'd *liked* what they'd seen enough to give their seal of approval and had rushed to tell him before it was too late. She'd hoped, but hadn't counted on marrying into a caring family. What joy it would be to have brothers around!

But a frown quickly marred her features. Though he was physically attracted to her, did Mr. Coltrain want her for his wife? Did she measure up in any way to *his* specifications?

Oblivious to the grasshoppers leaping in every direction, she lifted her gaze to the sky where giant thunderheads were clustering and hot gusts of wind whirled around her, blowing the curls off her forehead.

As her host had indicated earlier, there'd be a storm before the day was out. In her heart of hearts she hoped it would be of such intensity and duration, they wouldn't be able to get back to Wall tonight. He'd brought her here on a trial basis. She needed time to impress him that she'd make a proper wife.

Though they were only forty-five minutes from civilization, it intrigued her to pretend otherwise. Curious about everything, she walked around the side and caught sight of an outhouse maybe twenty feet away. Farther on, an ancient-looking tractor with an attached sickle mower met her gaze. The paint had long since worn off both pieces of machinery.

She wandered closer, intimately familiar with the unique designs, which bore the unmistakable stamp of her grandfather's engineering genius and explained why Mr. Coltrain was still getting the use out of them. High up on the tractor's steering column she saw the metal name plate. *Harrington.*

There probably wasn't a farmer or rancher in the entire United States who didn't own at least one piece of Harrington farming equipment manufactured out of Topeka, Kansas. Not even Mr. Coltrain was an exception....

A smile curved her lips. It pleased her to think that even before she'd come to Bad country, Xan and this rancher were already connected on at least one level. As far as she was concerned, it was a good omen.

"I know what you're thinking, ma'am, but you'd be wrong. Everything still runs." A deep voice spoke up behind her.

Schooling her features to show no emotion, she swung around to face him. "I'm not surprised. Most things made a long time ago were meant to last forever."

His eyes darkened to a cloudy green. As the uneasy silence stretched between them, she had a feeling she'd said the wrong thing again and couldn't account for it unless he thought she was patronizing him.

"Before the storm hits, I've got work to do. It would be best to get you settled inside first."

"Of course."

She followed him around the front of the house, observing his long stride. In spite of his work attire, which put her more in mind of a farmer, he possessed an understated air of aggression that challenged her and continually drew her interest.

But as she crossed over the threshold, her glance flicked momentarily to some weather-stained wooden doors, which obviously opened to a root cellar running near the foundation.

She paused, fascinated by everything she saw, then entered the stiflingly hot, airless house and waited for her eyes to adjust to the rectangular room, dimly lit by two kerosene lanterns.

The colorless, Spartan furnishings of a veritable pioneer museum greeted her vision. Except for the wooden plank floor—which seemed to be its only concession to modernization—everything looked authentic, down to an old wooden washtub propped against the far wall. Big enough for a man to bathe in...

In an attempt to blot certain disturbing pictures from her mind, her eyes took further inventory. At one end of the room near the hearth rested a handmade bed. A well-worn faded quilt had been hastily thrown over a straw-ticking mattress large enough to hold two small people. Mr. Coltrain would fill the whole thing. As for her joining him...

Experiencing a wave of heat that owed nothing to the elements, she quickly looked askance at an old wooden trunk set against the wall. Above it someone had built a set of shelves and a bar to hold clothes.

Another corner served as a storeroom for a shovel, pitchfork, ladder, broom and other ranching tools.

A tiny kitchen with a modest supply of stores placed on open shelving nestled on the other side of the room along with a cast iron cook stove and a pile of wood. He'd put her folded awning and the pastor's picnic basket on the counter.

In the center of the house sat a handmade wooden table and one rickety-looking wooden chair. Mr. Coltrain had placed her stool next to it.

For some reason, the sight of the bright red stool caused her throat to constrict with emotion. In a subtle way, the gesture seemed to say that he was entertaining serious thoughts about her. She sucked in her breath, praying that it was true.

Immediately her eye saw a myriad of possibilities. An easy chair and love seat, some flowers, a colored tablecloth, floral bedspread and braided rug could do wonders to create warmth without disturbing the original flavor of his home. Though there were no windows, she could imagine a pretty curtain to partition off the bedroom and create a little privacy.

If they were to marry, and *if* he would allow her to help him, it wouldn't have to take him ten years to pay off his loan.

Supposing they had a baby right away... Surely he'd let her use some of her money to have a couple of bedrooms added on, bedrooms with windows and stacks of wonderful books to read. *Their own little heaven on earth.*

"Feel free to make yourself at home, Ms. Harrington," he said in a deep, vibrant voice, startling her back to reality. "There's a pitcher pump over the sink where you can wash, but don't be tempted to drink the water. It comes from an underground cistern and isn't safe.

"If you get thirsty, you'll find a drum of potable water around the side of the house. Help yourself to that and the buffalo jerky over on the drain board. There are fruits and vegetables in the cellar, but you'd best leave everything to me. No telling what you'll find down there. And with this storm blowing in, there'll be jackalopes roaming about. You can't be too careful."

His gaze studied her features with such intensity, she didn't know what made her tremble more—his words, or the strange glitter in his eyes.

In a quiet aside he added, "I'll try to get home by dark and rustle us up some dinner."

On his way out, he reached inside the picnic basket for a fat slice of homemade bread and devoured it before he'd even had time to shut the door behind him.

She saw through his tactics. Ever since she'd met him, he'd deliberately tried to present the worst possible picture so that she'd know exactly what she was getting into if she married him. He figured the isolation, the deprivation, the heat, the bugs and the strange animals would be too much for her.

No doubt he expected her to run after him and beg him to take her back to town right now. But Xan had no such intention.

She loved his gut-wrenching honesty.

She loved *everything* about this strong, humble, hardworking rancher of few words and vowed to work her way into his heart no matter how long it took.

He'd passed every test.

Xan couldn't wait to phone May with the news that she was planning on becoming *Mrs. Amasa Judd Coltrain*.

CHAPTER FOUR

BY NINE-THIRTY that night, jagged bolts of lightning lit up the sky. Ferocious thunder followed, shaking the ground. Since dark, Xan had been listening for the sound of the tractor, but now that the storm front had moved in, she couldn't hear anything but the pounding of rain on the roof.

If Mr. Coltrain didn't return soon, she planned to go looking for him. Maybe the tractor had run out of gas and he needed help. She wouldn't allow herself to think about his getting struck by lightning and killed, like May's husband.

Thank heavens she'd thought to put plywood from her booth in the truck's window frames to keep out the rain. At least if she had to go out later, the cab wouldn't be completely soaked.

Staying busy helped keep her fears at bay. For the last eight hours she had worked hard to fix things as attractively as possible. After all, he'd told her to make herself at home, but perhaps in her zeal to show him she belonged here, she'd gone too far.

The thing is, she'd wanted to surprise him and had hoped he wouldn't return until everything was ready. But now it was long past the time for his arrival.

Her glance darted around the room that she'd swept and scrubbed until there was no more dust anywhere. Calling on her flair for decorating, she'd arranged the awning into an attractive tablecloth, and had found an eggshell tinted water pitcher to serve for a centerpiece.

She'd scrubbed it inside and out until it gleamed, then had filled it with fresh drinking water from the huge drum around the side of the house. Along with bits of cutlery and chipped pottery placed on the striped material, she felt her creation could pass inspection quite nicely.

The pastor had put some white napkins in the picnic basket. Since they hadn't been used yet, she slid one under each fork, and then set salt, pepper and honey on the table. Everything stood in readiness and dinner could be served at any time.

Throughout the day, she'd mentally praised May who, like all good Iowa farm wives, had taught Xan how to cook from scratch. With a little vegetable oil sitting on the shelf, she'd managed to stir up a nice skillet of carrots and potatoes for the main course, and an apple cobbler with dried raisins for dessert. Since there was no butter, Xan had been forced to improvise and knew May would be proud of her efforts. She could only hope Mr. Coltrain would be pleased.

After debating for over an hour, Xan had finally found the courage to go out to the cellar and face a prairie rattlesnake or a jackalope, because she knew Mr. Coltrain would be starving when he came home.

Opening the doors, she'd gingerly descended the wooden steps. With the aid of a lantern in one hand and an old bucket in the other, she'd begun her search for something to fix for their evening meal besides buffalo jerky and some leftover homemade bread.

The five-by-five space, taller than her head, felt at least forty degrees cooler than the air outside. She wasn't at all surprised to discover that among the gunnysacks of vegetables, there was an old bushel basket containing some red apples still crisp and delicious to the bite.

She filled the bucket with all the fruit, potatoes and carrots she could carry, then hurried up the stairs and inside the house to start dinner.

Once she got going, she decided to cook up a storm and made biscuits with the powdered milk she'd found on the shelf. Of course she'd had to throw out the first three batches learning how to regulate the heat from the stove. But now she was satisfied she could place golden brown biscuits before her rancher. As soon as he walked through the door, she'd put the last batch in the oven.

When everything was done, she combed her hair, washed her face and applied fresh lipstick. That's when she got the idea to fix him a hot bath. Nothing could be worse than getting trapped in pouring rain. He'd be soaked, muddy and exhausted.

It took close to fifteen minutes to pump the water, heat it and pour it into the tub, which she'd pulled close to the sink. He could use the hand soap on the drain board. Among his things she found *one* towel, which she laid over the back of the chair.

As she watched the steam rise, she realized there was nothing more to do. If Mr. Coltrain didn't come soon, his bath would grow cold and her dinner would be ruined.

But none of that mattered if he was in trouble, her heart warned.

She anxiously paced the floor, then made the decision to start up the truck and look for him. To her recollection, he'd left his keys in the ignition.

The rain hadn't stopped, but thankfully, the worst of the storm had passed over. She dashed outside, opened the truck door and climbed into the cab. Mindless of the grasshoppers lounging everywhere, she removed the plywood from the windows and started the engine.

After a minute or two, she turned on the headlights and the windshield wipers, then put the truck in gear. *Where to go first?*

He'd said that his house marked the beginning of his property, so she maneuvered onto the road and drove in the opposite direction from the way they'd come that morning.

It seemed like a century ago.

She felt like she was already a different person.

While she drove, she honked the horn, then waited and listened in case he called out to her. There was no response.

She couldn't have gone more than a mile when the motor started to sputter. Frustrated, she pressed on the gas. Nothing happened except that the truck came to a complete standstill. The dials had long since broken, but she didn't need a fuel gauge to tell her she'd run out of gas.

Furious that she'd left the house before making certain she carried some fuel with her, she turned off the lights to save the battery and jumped out of the truck. Maybe he kept a can in the back for emergencies.

The rain had stopped, but the darkness made it impossible to discern much of anything. Once she'd climbed over the tailgate, the bed of the truck appeared to be as messy as the front floor of the cab. She stumbled over slippery wet cables, feed bags, crates, another pitchfork, rags, even a small generator hidden beneath an old tarp. But as far as she could tell, there was no gas.

Suppressing her panic, she realized that the only thing she could do was head back to the house and hope the can she'd seen next to the water drum still had some gas in it.

Fearing that he would think her a complete fool, she took no thought for herself as she jumped off the side. But the second her right foot touched the ground, she felt her ankle twist, sending her flying headlong into the grass. The jolt made the world spin, and for a few minutes the pain with its attendant nausea rendered her immobile.

Xan had no idea how long she lay there, but eventually she got to her feet, wincing with every movement. She didn't think her ankle was broken, but she'd wrenched it severely enough that the thought of a mile's walk daunted her.

Clinging to the door in a cold sweat, she took several deep breaths, praying for inspiration.

When she didn't return, Mr. Coltrain would worry and probably feel responsible for her disappearance because he'd left her so long. Of course, that was assuming he'd *come* home.

What if he was out here somewhere lying helpless or unconscious? She couldn't bear the thought of it.

Disciplining herself not to feel her distress or think about wild animals, she started limping along the side of the muddy road, crying out in agony with every step. She'd only gone a few hundred yards when the pain grew too acute.

She sank down in the grass to rest her ankle. That's when she heard the unmistakable sounds of the tractor coming in her direction.

Joy and thanksgiving gave her the strength to get on her feet. "Mr. Coltrain?" she shouted at the top of her lungs. "I'm over here!"

"What in the devil?" she heard him mutter fiercely as he pulled to the side of the road.

She'd never been so happy to see anyone in her life and couldn't seem to stop babbling as he hurried over to her in a few swift strides, steadying her upper arms with his hands.

"Thank heavens you're all right!" she cried out emotionally, unaware for the moment of her own discomfort as his eyes took a thorough inventory of her pallor and condition.

Knowing he was safe produced such great relief, her body seemed to sway into his of its own volition. With a moan of satisfaction she nestled against his wet warmth where she felt his chest heave and heard the heavy thud of his heart.

She was too happy to have been found to worry about propriety or the grim lines bracketing his stern mouth, but he obviously had other things on his mind and forced her away from him, demanding, "Why wouldn't I be all right?"

She struggled for breath. "When it got so late, I was afraid that your tractor had broken down, or—" her voice faltered "—that you'd been struck by lightning, so I came out here to look for you, but the truck ran out of gas. I hurt my ankle when I jumped from the back of the truck. I'm sorry," she whispered, wishing she could see his eyes right now because their color changed with the state of his emotions and gave him away. "I know it was stupid to leave the house without making sure I had some extra gas. Please forgive me."

"You didn't run out of gas," he murmured in a barely recognizable voice. "The spark plugs are wet. By the time I get you back to the truck, it'll start up again."

As easily as he might wield a bale of hay, he picked her up in his arms and covered the short distance to the truck, accomplishing it in no time at all.

He put her down by the driver's side with exquisite gentleness. After opening the door, he reached in to settle the Sears catalogues over the springs.

"What's wet plywood doing on the seat?" he inquired as he moved the boards to the floor.

"I—I used it for windows so the rain wouldn't ruin the inside of your truck."

She watched him rake the hair off his forehead, almost as if he needed to leash his energy in some way. Then, without warning, he grasped her hips to lift her inside.

Like before, their bodies brushed against each other, only this time he seemed reluctant to let her go. Like a branding iron, she felt the pressure and heat of his hands through the thin material of her damp shorts.

The sensation brought a slight gasp to her lips. He must have heard it because she suddenly found herself free to maneuver across the seat to her side of the truck.

"H-how did you know where to find me?" she stammered in confusion as he got behind the wheel and shut the door.

After a tense period of silence he murmured, "I saw fresh tracks in the mud and followed them."

"You must have come home right after I left. I can just imagine what you must have thought when you discovered the truck missing."

He took a long time to respond. "No, Ms. Harrington, this is one time when I don't think you can."

On that cryptic note he turned the key in the ignition and gunned the accelerator repeatedly. After a few minutes the motor caught. He revved it a while, then backed the truck around so they were headed home.

"What about the tractor?"

She felt his weight shift, another indication that he was having trouble holding on to his control. "It can stay put until morning."

She *had* made him angry, and there was no one to blame but herself. "D-did you go inside the house first?" She might as well know all the bad news now, in case he was furious about her taking so many liberties in his absence.

There was another harsh intake of breath, then he said, "No, ma'am."

Deciding she'd better not say anything else, she turned her head away from him and looked out her window, inhaling deeply of the air, which smelled of the earth and cool, sweet Dakota grass—a wonderful smell she would always associate with the remarkable man sitting next to her and remember for the rest of her life.

Far too soon they arrived at the house. He swung the truck close to the front door and turned off the ignition.

After climbing out, he opened the door of the house, waited for her to inch herself across the seat, then once more gathered her against his chest.

Without saying a word, he nudged the truck door shut with his backside, then carried her over the soddy's threshold. But unlike earlier in the day, the glow from the polished lanterns illuminated the freshly cleaned room with its colorful table set for two and seemed to transform it.

Instead of hot, stale air, the delicious smell of home cooking, roast potatoes and apples greeted their nostrils.

After shutting the door with his boot, a tangible stillness came over Mr. Coltrain, who paused right where he was with her grasped in his arms. Excited and anxious all at the same time, she tried to hold herself away from him, hoping he wouldn't detect the frantic beating of her heart.

Beneath her dark lashes she eyed his dominant profile covertly, watching as his gaze traveled slowly around the room, assessing the subtle changes a woman could achieve, changes that transferred a house into a home.

Like someone in a trance, he edged closer to the kitchen area and stopped in front of the tub. With her still pressed against his heart, he leaned over and put a finger in the water.

"For me?" he whispered huskily, at last bestowing the full blaze of his impossibly green eyes on her.

She nodded, too bemused by the nearness of his sensuous mouth and the incredulous expression on his face to find words.

His chest inflated as if he was having a difficult time containing his emotions. "Well, now, I have to admit I didn't expect matters to move ahead quite this fast."

She blinked. "This fast?"

"Yes, ma'am. I figure I've finally found the woman God picked out for me. Judging from all the trouble you've gone to, you must feel the same way. Am I right?''

The loaded question hung in the air like a living thing, causing her pulse rate to triple.

"You're hesitating, ma'am. I suppose that's only natural on account of the fact that there's still one more test to go. The most important one, as I see it." His voice grated.

Then the thing happened she'd been waiting for since they'd met last night. He lowered his head and covered her mouth with his own, blotting out the world and everything in it except this intensity of feeling that had her clinging to him, never wanting him to stop. First one kiss, then another and another, each one deeper, more provocative than the one before as they found delight in the taste and feel of each other.

Like a voracious hunger that had never been appeased until now, Xan couldn't get enough of him. It never occurred to her to hold back or refuse what he, too, wanted so desperately. There was honesty in everything he said and did, which explained why he held nothing back now and gave to her as she didn't think possible.

Dear God. To live with a man like this—a man who could make her feel like this until the end of their days—

From the tenor of his breathing, he was experiencing the same heart-stopping ecstasy. When he started to lower her to the floor, she felt he was reading her mind. They needed to be closer. Much closer. But she'd forgotten about her ankle, and when her foot came in contact with the planking, she let out a cry.

His head reared back far enough for her to witness the glazed look of desire in his eyes. "What's wrong?" The question came out on a hoarse whisper.

She swallowed hard because the pain in her extremity echoed the throbbing of her body. Her entire being was on fire. "My ankle," she murmured, out of breath.

Again she felt that odd stillness come over him. He let her go long enough to reach for the stool so she could sit. Then he got down on his haunches to investigate.

She was about to tell him which leg, but it appeared no explanation was necessary because the swelling on the outside of her right ankle was clearly visible.

He tenderly probed her injury, much the same as he might examine the leg of an injured horse. Everything he did bespoke his expertise and experience, endearing him to her all the more.

The next thing she knew he pulled the stool next to the tub, removed her sandals and plunged her muddy legs in the water, which had long since cooled.

"Oh, but this water was for you so you could have a nice bath!" she protested and tried to remove them, but he shook his dark head.

"It's the thought that counts, ma'am."

Reaching for the soap, he washed her shapely limbs, sending a delicious warmth through her body with every brush of his fingers.

Sighing, she said, "That feels good on my sprain."

His sober gaze eventually trapped hers. The way he was looking at her now, the passion they'd shared a moment ago might never have been. Except that one of his hands was still cupping her calf, like he was memorizing its shape. "You're lucky you didn't break your ankle."

Chastened, she averted her eyes. "I know. It was too dark and my toe plunged into a hole of some kind. But that's all over now and it's you who needs waiting on. You're dinner's all ready except for the biscuits that have to go in the oven."

Almost as if he was reluctant, he released her leg and got to his feet. "If you'll stay put, I reckon I can finish things up."

For the next few minutes she relaxed while she watched him light the stove and get dinner under way. His economy of movement, the sureness of his actions, his confidence, everything about him absorbed her, assured her, as no other man had ever done before.

Already she felt like they were husband and wife, sharing the good with the bad at the end of a busy day.

She never wanted to leave him, not even to go back to Wall for her things. In all honesty, she was feeling extremely territorial about him.

The pastor had talked about a lot of eligible females who'd like to trade places with her right now. Well, possession was nine-tenths of the law, and she was *here*, breaking bread with him, as May put it. Spending the night ought to put the seal on everything.

"That's a mighty pretty table you set, Ms. Harrington," he said as he took the biscuits out of the oven. "Seems a shame not to enjoy it, but you're better off getting the heat out of that ankle."

So saying, he handed her a full plate, then drew up the chair next to her and tucked in to his own dinner with unfeigned relish.

By now she was starving and ate everything much too fast. Not one to brag, she thought it was the best meal she'd ever tasted and held her breath, waiting for him to say something.

After three helpings of potatoes and cobbler, followed by six biscuits, which he devoured in no time at all, he claimed he was full, took their plates over to the counter and started making coffee.

When he asked if she'd like some, she declined. His mere presence acted on her adrenal glands. She didn't need another stimulant to accelerate her heartbeat.

Instead of sitting next to her, he lounged against the counter with one leg crossed over the other at the ankle. Above the rim of his cup, he stared hard at her.

She could tell he'd come to an important decision. Afraid she might not have passed all *his* tests, she started to panic and stirred restlessly on the stool.

"I'll be blunt, Ms. Harrington. I don't want to drive you back to Wall tonight."

"I—I don't want to go.' The comment slipped out of its own accord. She couldn't take it back.

His narrowed glance captured hers. "The problem is, if we spend the night together, the pastor'll know all about it by morning."

She looked down at the water. "Though he was nice about it, he already thinks I'm a Jezebel. I don't suppose my reputation could get much worse than that."

After digesting her comment he said, "I think you missed my point, ma'am. He'll be so delighted, he'll want to marry us as soon as possible."

Her heart skipped a beat.

Was this his unique way of proposing to her?

He never did things like other men. Since honesty seemed to be a part of the day, she decided to go all the way. "Do you?" she whispered, trying to see into his soul. "Want to m-marry me, I mean?" Her voice shook.

He lowered his cup to the counter and folded his arms across his broad chest. "A woman who looks like you, kisses like you, cooks like you, is almost too good to be true.

"Yes, ma'am. I want to marry you, probably more than anything I ever wanted in my whole life, but I have to keep asking myself if you're for real." After a brief pause he said, "Are you sure you want to marry me and live out here year after year under adverse conditions, taking whatever God sends us?''

Struggling for breath she said, ''If you mean children, I can hardly wait. I was an only child and it was a pretty lonely existence. I want a houseful. H-how do you feel about children?''

He cocked his head. ''Naturally I'd like to raise some sons and daughters, but only with the right woman.''

''I feel the same way.''

''If you're the kind who gets pregnant easily, this house could burst at the seams before we're through.''

Blushing, Xan was already way ahead of him, but until the time was right, she decided to keep her own counsel. ''I can't imagine anything more wonderful.''

''Well, ma'am—'' His eyes glittered with a strange light. ''The only thing I see left is to meet your people.''

''There's only May. I'll phone her. She can fly out at any time so the two of you can get acquainted. I'm just as anxious to meet your brothers. I want to thank them for their part in getting us together. As soon as May arrives, why don't we all have dinner in town. Maybe the pastor and his wife can join us, a-and any of your close friends, if you'd like.''

He straightened to his full height. ''I think I'd prefer our first meeting to be for family only.''

''Anything is fine with me.''

''I can't give you a ring.''

If only he knew.

She shook her head and looked him straight in the eye. "Believe me when I tell you that a ring means nothing to me. Marrying the right man is all I care about. I want to marry you, Mr. Coltrain," she stated solemnly, knowing in her heart of hearts it was true.

She'd found her Bad man and was prepared to surmount any obstacle to belong to him.

CHAPTER FIVE

"IF THERE isn't anything else you need, I'm turning off the lanterns now."

In the dark, she could hear him changing his clothes. He'd long since washed the dishes and carried her to the outhouse. Then he'd helped her to bed. While her pounding heart suffocated her, Xan lay on the uncomfortable mattress still dressed in her shorts and blouse, a damp rag fastened around her ankle to keep down the swelling.

"Where will you sleep tonight?"

"With you, ma'am. I thought I'd made that fact perfectly clear."

"B-but I don't think there's room."

"We'll work something out."

"Mr. Coltrain, you might as well know right now that I've never slept with a man before."

"In other words, you'd rather we waited until our wedding night."

She never knew anyone so baldly frank, yet it was one of the qualities she loved most about him. "Yes. I'm not asking for myself. It's for May. I promised her to remain chaste until I said my marriage vows."

After a short silence he said, "In that case, I'll

tell the pastor we want to be married next Saturday. I won't be able to wait any longer than that. Do you think May can make it out here in time?''

Her thoughts reeled. "Yes, of course. If you drive me back to Wall in the morning, I'll phone her straight away and she'll arrange for her flight.''

"Since you shouldn't be on that leg, I'll drive into town, pick up your things from the motel and make the call for you.''

Her eyes closed tightly. *Oh, please, May. Please don't give me away. Not yet.*

"That's probably a better idea,'' she whispered shakily. "Otherwise the pastor will tell everyone in sight I'm the Jezebel who had to limp to the altar to hog-tie her man.''

Deep, unrestrained laughter rumbled out of Mr. Coltrain. Maybe it was the dark that made him sound so different than the man she thought she knew. A little shiver washed over her skin as he drew near.

"Whatever story he tells, word will go out that you're the most beautiful sight to ever grace his church.''

Before she could respond with any coherence, he eased himself over her body and lay down on the mattress next to her.

"I—I thought—''

"Relax, ma'am. I made you a promise. I'd never go back on it. But I never promised not to hold you. There are still things we need to learn about each other. If one of us has a snoring problem, we'll have to deal with it.''

"Snoring!" she cried out in horror, because it was something she'd never thought about before. "I don't know if I snore or not."

He chuckled near her ear. "Don't worry about it. If you do, I'll just buy me a couple of earplugs."

"Or not marry me at all," she said, half in fear he might back out if she did.

"Let's get something straight,' he murmured into her dark curls, putting his arm around her waist and drawing her back so she could feel the hard length and breadth of him through his clean overalls. "Nothing and no one could make me back out now.

"For thirty-seven years I've been dreaming about a woman who'd live on this land with me. A woman who looks like you, who smells as sweet and feels as good. How about a good-night kiss?"

"I—I don't think that would be a good idea," she lamented, wishing with every fiber of her being that she dared. But May had raised her to respect her body, and Xan knew that if they started kissing, they wouldn't stop. In fact, she wondered how much longer she could lie nestled against him without going out of her mind.

"Your self-control is admirable, Ms. Harrington. Unfortunately, mine isn't that good and I need more from you or I'll never get to sleep. Shall I move to your other side, or are you going to make this easy and turn toward me?"

Xan had no defense against his desire or her own. More than eager, she rolled in his direction, careful not to jar her ankle too much.

"That's more like it," he whispered against her lips, his soft facial hair brushing against her heated skin. Then they were kissing again, hungrily.

This was heaven. Nothing in life could ever touch what was happening to her now. She had no words to describe the feelings coming to life inside of her. Finally she'd found out where she belonged. It was in this man's arms, her legs tangled with his, their hearts wildly beating against each other.

To her shame, he was the one who finally tore his lips from hers, ending the rapture so abruptly she moaned in agony.

With the speed and stealth of a panther, he levered himself off the bed, managing to keep from touching her. "You were right," he said in an oddly strained voice. All the playfulness of his earlier mood had disappeared.

"A man ought to be able to keep a promise to the woman he's about to marry. But I hadn't counted on you being quite so desirable. The simple truth is, if I stay in that bed with you any longer, I'll have to break my promise, and that's another promise."

His admission thrilled her. "W-where will you sleep?"

"In the truck. I've done it before."

"But you're too tall, and those springs—"

"I'll get out my bedroll and sleep in the back."

"But the back's a mess."

"That's why I need a wife."

"You do. As soon as my ankle's better, I'll tackle your truck and make it look nice. Mr. Coltrain— do you mind if I call you by your first name?"

"No, ma'am."

"Then will you please call me Xan? Ma'am is a very polite word, but it makes me feel old."

"I've been waiting for you to give me permission. Is Xan your legal name?"

She took a deep breath. "No. I don't like the one my parents gave me."

"Are we going to have secrets even before we're married?" he drawled.

She flushed guiltily and was grateful for the darkness. "No. I—it's Roxanne."

"Roxanne." He said the word experimentally. "It's exotic. No woman around these parts has a name like it."

"I know. That's why I don't like it."

"When our first daughter comes along, she'll probably be a real beauty, just like you. We can call her Roxy."

Xan's heart turned over. "I always planned that if I ever had a little girl, I'd call her Roxy."

"If we have a boy first, we won't call him Judd. I want that clear right now."

"That's fine because I already have his name picked out."

She heard a slight hesitation before he said, "What's that?"

"Cole. It should have been your name."

"Is that right?"

"Yes."

"Well, if we have a son, I guess we can try it on him. Good night, Xan."

"Good night, Judd."

Mrs. Judd Coltrain.

Ecstatic, she closed her eyes and turned her face into the pillow, more and more convinced that an unseen hand had guided her to South Dakota, to this exact spot, to this exact Bad man.

With him guarding the house she felt safe and protected against any intruders, human or otherwise, and fell asleep with her head full of plans to make him so happy, he'd never regret marrying her.

The excitement of everything must have made her more tired than she'd realized, because according to her watch, she didn't wake up until ten the next morning.

Shocked at the time, she quickly sat up, noting that Judd had come in earlier. Out of consideration, he'd left a lantern burning on the table so she wouldn't have to stagger around a dark room.

Was he off bringing the tractor back, or had he already gone to town? If so, he'd left without getting her phone number so he could call May.

Throwing back the quilt, she carefully placed her feet on the floor to unwrap her bandage and discovered another surprise. He'd put her sandals next to the bed. They looked new. No one seeing them would believe they'd been caked with mud last night.

His thoughtfulness continually amazed her and made her want to give him everything in return.

Favoring her right leg, she got to her feet and slid into her sandals. Though the swelling had gone down during the night, her ankle was still painful. She'd definitely be limping for a while.

Thankful for a small house, she took her time traversing the room, noticing that he'd emptied the tub and put it back against the wall.

Out of the corner of her eye, she saw a piece of paper on the table next to the lantern. He must have torn it out of one of the catalogues in the truck. She picked it up and read it.

Dear Xan, have gone into town and should be back by early afternoon. There's cocoa on the shelf, jerky and biscuits from last night. I'll be bringing back more supplies.

I took the liberty of opening your purse and getting the information I needed from your driver's license to call May. Please don't take that action wrong. In your ad, you said you wanted a man you could share everything with, so I took you at your word. I suppose I should have wakened you, but you were in such a deep sleep, I didn't have the heart to disturb you.

If you want to know the truth, you've made me a very happy man. You're just as beautiful asleep as you are awake, and you don't snore, which is a good thing since earplugs drown out all the sound. I wouldn't know if a jackalope was around or not.

Stay off that foot.

Judd.

Xan must have read his note a dozen times before she put it down. Elation over the prospect of marrying him made her slightly giddy. *Now if May would only do her part.*

Obeying the call of nature, she limped from the house and made a quick visit out back, where he'd parked the tractor once more. He must have gotten up at the crack of dawn!

It was a glorious morning, no clouds, just prairie and sky. Of course the sun was out, and before long the heat would be atrocious and the grasshoppers would be leaping. But right now the air was still fresh from the rain, and Xan was happier than she'd ever been in her life.

Halfway around the house, she heard the sound of a motor. Someone was coming down the road. *Judd?*

As she rounded the corner, she caught sight of a brand new Blazer pulling up in front with the words Lazy L Ranch painted on the sides.

Two attractive men got out. They were dressed in expensive-looking Stetsons and Western-cut suits. They both saw her at the same time and strode toward her. Something about the way they walked, their features, told her they were Judd's younger brothers.

Immediately she wondered what had happened in their family that Judd should have to struggle so hard to earn his living, when it was apparent his brothers lacked for nothing.

"Good morning," they both said, removing their hats. The elder of the two—probably in his early thirties—spoke first. "I'm Lon Coltrain, and he's Kenneth. In case Judd hasn't told you about us yet, we're his brothers."

Xan nodded. "I know all about you. The three of you share a strong family resemblance."

They both grinned. "Are we right in assuming you're Ms. Harrington?"

"You *know* you're right." She smiled warmly and reached out to shake hands with them. "I'm glad you're here. I wanted the opportunity to thank you for showing him my ad. If it hadn't been for you, Judd and I would never have met."

Ken, the one who looked to be in his mid-twenties, eyed his brother and winked.

Xan liked them on sight and wished she didn't feel at such a disadvantage. Her blouse and shorts were wrinkled, her hair hadn't been brushed, and Judd had kissed away any lipstick she'd been wearing. She'd been trying hard not to think about his kisses because every time she did, she couldn't breathe.

Lon, the taller of the two, gazed at her speculatively, reminding her of Judd. "We've been looking everywhere for him. Do you know where he is?"

"Yes. He's gone to town for supplies, but he said he'd be back after lunch. Would you like to come in and wait for him?"

Lon said, "There's nothing we'd like better. Ken, get on the cellular phone and call the ranch. Tell them where we are, that we've located Judd."

"Will do."

While Ken complied with his brother's bidding, Lon followed Xan.

"What's wrong with your leg?" he asked when he saw her limping through the grass.

"I sprained my ankle. It's kind of a long story."

"That's a shame." He offered his arm for her to lean on. "When did it happen?"

"Last night."

He frowned. "What's the matter with Judd bringing you clear out here? And why didn't he take you to see a doctor?"

"I asked to come," she said, defending him. "Besides, my sprain wasn't that serious," she murmured, somewhat hurt by Lon's attitude. Just because Judd didn't have money and a prosperous ranch didn't mean he had anything to be ashamed of.

After pondering her comments he said, "Well, this has to be a first for him."

Her heart started to race. "You mean he's never brought another woman out here?"

By this time, Ken had caught up with them.

"Hey, Kenny? Do you ever recall Judd bringing a woman all the way out here before?"

"Are you kidding?" Ken barked.

His answer made Xan's happiness complete. But she didn't want them to get the wrong idea. As they crossed over the threshold she volunteered, "He soaked my ankle and made a compress for it, then slept in the back of his truck last night so I could use his bed. As you can see, I'm much better this morning."

Like Judd had done the night before, the two brothers went perfectly still. She didn't know if it was because of what she'd said or because of what they were looking at. For the longest time their eyes took inventory of the interior.

"I—I was just about to fix some hot chocolate and warm up some biscuits I made last night. Would you like to join me for a late breakfast?"

Lon's puzzled gaze swerved to hers. "You made biscuits for Judd last night? *Here?*"

"On that old monstrosity?" Ken asked her disbelievingly. "Hell, my wife can't even cook anything decent in the microwave."

"At least your wife tries," Lon muttered.

"The stove may be old, but it still works," Xan responded more primly than she'd intended. After being around his disapproving brothers, no wonder Judd had been afraid for her to see his place. "I'd offer you some apple cobbler, but it looks like Judd finished off the rest of it this morning before he left."

By tacit agreement they all moved over to the table, which was still set from last night. She saw Lon's eyes dart to the note Judd had left. Trying not to seem obvious, she removed it, folded it and slipped it into the pocket of her shorts. Suggesting that they sit down, she lit the stove and started making cocoa.

Ken fingered the tablecloth. "Where did Judd find this?"

Irritated because she felt he was making fun of Judd, she said, "Actually, the stool and awning are from my booth. He dismantled it for me and put everything in the truck. I decided it would make a nice covering, and we needed another place to sit."

By now Lon had perched himself on the chair and was staring at her. "We didn't mean to offend you, Ms. Harrington," he said in a sincere tone of voice. "It's just that Judd's never done anything like this before. We'd almost given up hope of him marrying. Then we got one look at you and figured you just might be the one. But he's gone and ruined his chances."

"The thing is," Ken interjected, "bringing you out here was just plain crazy. Now you'll never choose him."

"But I did," she admitted in a fit of pique. Maybe she shouldn't have said anything without Judd's permission, but they'd made her so mad, she didn't care. "We settled everything last night."

"What?" they both cried in unison. Ken was so surprised, he fell off the stool. Lon shook his head as if he didn't believe her.

"We're getting married next Saturday," she continued in a voice May would recognize as Xan's stubborn tone. "We've worked out most of the details with Pastor Swan. We've even planned our honeymoon. After that, we'll settle down and raise a family. If you must know, we've already decided on names for our children."

At this point Lon was on his feet, his expression one of shock. "Do you swear before God that what you're telling us is the truth?"

She lifted her chin in disdain. "Are you so distrustful of your brother you need me to swear an oath?" Her voice rang throughout the house.

A long silence followed while the two brothers stared at each other, digesting her outcry.

Ken was the first to respond. "Thank heavens our brother had the brains to grab you up before any of the other candidates beat him to it! I'm so happy I hardly know what to say, Ms. Harrington."

She could feel her heart thawing. "The name is Xan."

"Welcome to the family, Xan."

"Amen," Lon chimed in, sounding positively euphoric. "Wait till our wives hear about this. They'll throw you the biggest party this side of the Black Hills."

Suddenly they were embracing her with such heartfelt affection, she knew their feelings were genuine. She found herself hugging them back, hardly able to believe these men were going to become her brothers.

"Maybe you shouldn't say anything to anyone yet," she finally cautioned, and urged them to sit down to drink their hot chocolate. "Judd made it clear that for now he just wants family around. I think he'd better be the one to make our announcement official."

"Don't worry," Ken muttered. "Some time ago we learned not to tangle with Judd when it comes to his women."

"Were there a lot of them?" she asked without thinking, her jealousy getting the better of her.

Lon cleared his throat. "Let's just say that over the years, hundreds have tried, but failed."

Hundreds? "W-why did they fail?"

"Though she insisted it wasn't true, Judd was always Mother's favorite. He had to take over everything after Dad died, and of course, he more or less worshiped the ground she walked on. There were a couple of women who came close to catching him, but I guess even they didn't quite measure up." He beamed at Xan, his green eyes reminiscent of Judd's. "That is, until he met you."

"That's right." Lon corroborated Ken's explanation. "The thing is, that list of qualities you put in your ad? If you'd changed the wording to Bad Woman Wanted, you could have been talking about our mother. That's what we know got to Judd in the first place."

"That, and then seeing you."

"We were afraid he wouldn't show up at your booth."

Xan leaned against the counter, sipping her hot chocolate. "We almost missed each other. When he appeared, it was after ten and I was ready to leave the rodeo grounds."

"You should have put your picture with the ad. He'd have been your first candidate."

She shook her head. "Pictures can be deceiving. It's what's inside that counts."

Lon took exception. "That isn't altogether true. I mean you have to like what you see if you're going to live with that person forever."

"I agree," Xan admitted grudgingly, thinking that Lon sounded a lot like Judd just then.

"You're so gorgeous, my wife Stacey is going to be jealous," Ken commented.

"Let's face it, Kenny. She and Joanna and every woman who ever wanted to become Mrs. Judd Coltrain are going to hate it when they see who finally caught him."

The pastor's words to the letter. "Thank you," Xan whispered, deeply moved by their compliments. "However, I have to tell you that I'm the one who's lucky because I'm inheriting two wonderful brothers along with a husband."

"You don't have any brothers?"

"No." Then she proceeded to explain about her background.

"Well, we didn't have any sisters, so this is just as exciting for us. Where—"

But Xan wasn't destined to hear what Ken was on the point of asking because Judd unexpectedly entered the house, breaking up what probably looked to him like a very cozy session. Both brothers rushed over to him with grins on their faces, patting him on the back. "Congratulations, brother."

His gaze flicked to Xan who felt distinctly uncomfortable at being the one who'd told them the news before he did. "I—I hope you don't mind," she said, her eyes pleading with him.

From the distance separating them, she couldn't read any emotion on his face. "The only thing I mind is that neither one of my brothers was gentleman enough to let you sit down with that bad ankle. I thought our mother had taught them better manners than that.''

In a lightning move he reached her side, picked her up in his arms and carried her over to the bed. ''They should have been waiting on *you*, not the other way around,'' he murmured, tantalizing her with the brush of his lips before he straightened and sent them a speaking glance.

Xan could have laughed at the shocked looks on their faces. Either they weren't used to seeing Judd display his affection or he'd made them feel guilty.

Probably the latter, because Ken scuffed the toe of his cowboy boot against the floor and Lon said, ''Sorry, Judd. I guess we were so happy to hear the news, we weren't thinking too clearly.''

''Well, since that's nothing new, and since you two don't seem to have anything better to do than follow me around, I'll make it easy for you. Xan's obviously told you we're getting married on Saturday. I've got the ceremony fixed for two o'clock.''

If that was true, and he'd already talked to May, then that meant May had said all the right things when Judd had called her. Xan's relief knew no bounds.

''But there's something I want understood,' he asserted in a commanding tone. ''No one is allowed but family. Naturally I'll want both of you to stand up for me.''

Still looking astonished, Lon said, ''Of course, Judd. We've been waiting for this day for a long time.''

"I know you have."

"Can we tell everybody?"

"Sure you can, Kenny. Why don't you run an announcement in the *Rapid City Journal* on Sunday? That way the news will come out while Xan and I are on our honeymoon. We've decided to do our courting after the ceremony instead of before, so we'd like our privacy."

Ken frowned. "But this is going to be the biggest wedding of the decade. You can't cheat everyone out of that."

"There'll be plenty of time for parties *after* we get back. The thing is, we might take longer than normal because we need some time to get really acquainted. I figure the best wedding present you can give us is to do all my chores for me while we're gone."

Both brothers swallowed hard. "Sure. Anything you want."

Xan had it in her heart to feel sorry for them. Judd's idea of chores probably daunted most ranchers. Since his brothers knew him better than anyone, more than likely they were petrified at the prospect.

"That's good, because I need the acreage north of here plowed by the time we get back, and I figured that while you're at it, you could make a place for a garden along the side of the house."

"A garden?"

"Here?"

Xan raised questioning eyes to Judd, who stood looking at her with a curious light in those grass-green depths. "My wife-to-be is a beautiful woman and should have beautiful things around her. It seems to me that some flowers would make her happiest. Am I right?" he whispered in a thick voice.

As she continued looking at him, her eyes filled and she felt a sharp twinge in the region of her heart.

I'm in love with him, she realized. *Irrevocably.*

Both Ken and Lon were saying something, but for the life of her she had no idea what it was. Trapped by feelings that were so new and precious she hadn't had time to explore them yet, she could only watch in a kind of blurred daze as Judd suddenly wheeled away from her and ushered his brothers out the door.

CHAPTER SIX

"MAY! Over here!" Xan shouted.

Above the din of the crowd swarming around the deplaning passengers at the Rapid City airport, May's warm brown eyes found Xan's. They both ran toward each other at the same time.

"Lovey!" The slim, older woman hugged Xan fiercely before examining her with an intensity that didn't overlook a detail. "I've missed you, you know that?"

Xan's eyes misted, loving this woman who, for all intents and purposes, *was* her mother. "I've missed you, too," she cried, hugging her just as hard. "Come on." She linked her arm through May's. "Let's get your luggage."

"Where's the rancher who managed to steal my little girl away from me so fast I think I'm still dreaming? He may have been charming enough over the phone and said all the right things, but I want to see him in person. I'm not sure I trust him. Everything has happened much too fast."

"That's not true," Xan countered as they drew up to the baggage claim and watched for May's maroon-colored suitcase. "You told me that within five minutes of meeting John, you wanted to belong to him."

"But we didn't marry for six months."

Xan tightened her grip on May's arm. "Judd and I couldn't wait that long."

May's eyes narrowed. "You haven't—"

"No," Xan rushed to assure her, a blush creeping into her cheeks. In a shaky voice she confessed, "But staying away from him has been the hardest thing I've ever had to do in my life."

Her eyebrows quirked. "That bad?"

Xan bit her lip and nodded. "Thank heavens the ceremony is tomorrow. I don't think I could hold out any longer. Right now Judd is letting me use his bed while he sleeps in the truck. Which reminds me. He's waiting outside for us."

"Why didn't he come in?"

"He wanted to, but I told him that since he's saving every penny to pay off his ranch, there's no need to spend money for parking. The thing is, his truck is in terrible shape. You'll have to sit on some catalogues so the springs won't poke you. Just pretend you don't notice."

While they waited for her bag to show up on the carousel, May treated Xan to a soul-searching appraisal, which caused the younger woman to avert her eyes. "If he's that down-and-out, why haven't you bought him a new one?"

Staring at the ground Xan said, "He's quite old-fashioned, which is one of the things I love about him. I think he's the type of man determined to be the sole breadwinner. I'm afraid I would offend him if I offered to help out monetarily."

After an uncomfortable pause she heard May say, "Roxanne Harrington. You mean to tell me he still doesn't know who you are?"

"No."

She could feel May's disappointment.

"Shame on you. I kept your secret because I figured you would have told him the truth by now. What happened to the girl I raised to be honest in *all* her dealings?"

A guilty shudder wracked Xan's body. "You don't understand."

"Oh, I understand all right."

"No, May. You don't. Something has gone wrong for him. His brothers have money. *He's* the one struggling and needs to make it on his own. It's a male pride thing. I—I'll tell him when the time is right."

"There'll never be a right time unless you come forward *now*! After the wedding, it'll be too late. The more I hear about him, the more I'm convinced he's the kind of man who could handle anything *except* a lie.

"You're playing with fire and you're going to get hurt. Why not admit you've made a mistake and let's go home. I know you're not interested in Todd, but there are dozens of good men where you work. If you'd only give one of them a chance."

"I can't, May. I don't trust them."

"It's your grandfather's fault," May grumbled. "He's the one who made you like this."

"I'm glad. Otherwise I would never have met Judd."

Forcing Xan to face her, May said, "Look at me." When Xan did her bidding, May searched her eyes for a long time. "He means this much to you already?"

"I'm in love with him." Xan's voice throbbed with emotion. "When you meet him, you'll see why. He's unique, one of a kind. And he thrills me."

"It's the thrill part that concerns me," May objected with dogged determination. "When the thrills are gone, then what?"

"They'll never be over for me. Every time he touches me or looks at me, it's like the first time." Her voice caught. "Oh, please don't be this way, May," Xan begged.

"I can't help it, lovey. What you've done is just plain crazy! Throwing a dart at some board and coming up with a husband after only seven days of being here?" She shook her head.

"How can I make you understand, May? We both feel exactly the same way!"

"I have no doubts that *he* does. You're a great beauty, and the man lucky enough to win you will thank his lucky stars that there's substance to go along with those fabulous looks of yours. But a week isn't enough time to know what *you're* getting into."

"But May, don't you see? He took me out to his ranch. He forced me to face everything so I'd know exactly what to expect. He's made no promises or excuses and is the most humble man I've ever known. The pastor who's going to marry us adores him. So do his brothers. What more do I need to know?"

"Plenty." May flung the word at her. "Sometimes things change when you say, 'I do.'" She threw up her hands. "I concede that maybe this Judd is everything you think he is. But not even the pastor knows what goes on behind locked doors. Once you're alone with this man, he might turn out to be someone quite different."

"In what way?" Xan questioned in a hurt voice. She hated it when May made sense.

"For one thing, when he phoned me, I found out he's ten years older than you are. Any man who has been alone thirty-eight years is set in his ways. You'll have to make all the concessions."

"I don't mind."

"I do. A man like that could stamp out your spirit, rob you of your identity, especially if you're afraid to meet him on equal terms."

"I'm not afraid."

"Sure you are. Otherwise he'd know you're one of the wealthiest women in North America. I'd feel a lot better if I knew that *he* knew what you're worth. At least that way, I'd understand his motives better."

"He's the oldest of three brothers and had to look after them *and* his mother *and* the ranch after his father died," Xan said, defending Judd.

"If he's so wonderful, then how come he's the only one struggling now?"

Xan drew in a deep breath, wanting the answer to that question herself. "He hasn't volunteered any information yet, but I can assure you he has no motives beyond wanting a wife with the same qualities I'm looking for in a husband."

"You don't know that, and neither do I."

Afraid she was fighting a losing battle, Xan asked, "Are you worried he might hurt me? Is that what has made you so negative?"

For the first time, May's eyes shifted away. "Maybe. You never know about a man who takes a defenseless woman to live in some remote spot."

"You did that with John!"

"Yes, after getting well acquainted for half a year first."

"So what are you saying? You want me to wait six months?"

"Would that be such a terrible thing? Surely if he's the one for you, then putting off the wedding a little longer will show whether both your feelings can stand the test of time. I know I'll sleep better at night."

Xan was devastated. "I don't think he'll want to wait."

"Then he couldn't love you enough."

"That's not fair!"

May's eyes dimmed. "Lovey—I'm only trying to say what I feel your parents would say if they were alive. It's your life and I won't interfere, but I can't pretend to like the situation. There's something wrong with a man who has remained a bachelor so many years all of a sudden wanting to get married this fast!"

"But he doesn't know about my money."

"Roxanne." She sounded weary. "How many times have I told you, there could be worse things than being wanted for your money! At least with Todd, you wouldn't experience too many unpleasant surprises."

"What are you getting at?" Xan demanded, feeling herself on the verge of tears.

The older woman lowered her head, defeated. "I don't know. It's just a feeling."

Suddenly Xan thought she understood. "May, there hasn't been enough time to discuss everything yet, but I planned to buy you a house and hoped you would move to Wall and make new friends here at the church so we could always be together." She reached out to hug the other woman. "I couldn't stand it if we had to live so far apart.

"I want you to share in the rest of my life and Judd's, and be a grandma to our children. Who knows? *You* might even meet a man to love. There are dozens of eligible ranchers around here. Wonderful men. But until then, it's my turn to take care of you. I love you."

"I love you, too, and there's nothing I'd like better." She sniffed. "But I think your husband-to-be might have something to say about that, so let's not get ahead of oursel— Oh, there are my cases!"

"Two of them?" Xan murmured in surprise as they each reached for one.

"Your mother's wedding dress is in the garment bag you're holding."

My mother's wedding dress?

Xan was so moved, so touched, she couldn't say anything and simply raised tear-drenched eyes to May, whose mouth curved in a wistful smile.

"Well, I couldn't let my little girl walk down the aisle in anything else, could I?"

"I—I didn't know of its existence. Oh, May!" She flung her arms around the older woman, her emotions too raw to find words.

Everything would be all right now.

"Come on, lovey." May was the first to break them up. "Let's go outside so I can meet this paragon of yours."

Xan nodded and wiped her eyes. "You'll love him."

Together they left the terminal and met a wall of late-afternoon heat. Xan steered them through the throng of people toward the truck lined up with a long string of cars parked against the curb. Judd had gotten out and was chatting with an airport security guard several yards away.

"Goodness gracious. Will you look at that splendid specimen of a man!" May murmured in awe. "But his overalls must be as old as the *Farmer's Almanac*! You can't help but wonder what he'd look like in normal clothes."

Xan's thoughts exactly! A smile lit her face. Judd had already made his impact on May, and his clothes were the least of it. "I told you he was old-fashioned," she whispered excitedly.

May wheeled around, astonishment crinkling her features. "*He's* your Bad man?"

"Yes. I can't wait for you to meet him."

They were too far away for Judd to have heard Xan, but he must have sensed her presence because he unexpectedly turned in her direction.

No matter how many times his penetrating gaze roamed over her face and body, her heart ran away with her. "Judd? Meet May Latta," she said in a breathless voice, "my only family. I've already asked her to move to Wall to be near us."

"Ma'am," he replied, extending his hand to May. "It's a pleasure to meet the person who raised Xan to be a perfect lady, just like my mother. I'm counting the minutes until she's my wife."

Xan nearly fainted from the ring of possession in his deep voice.

"I have to admit I've been curious about the man who in one short week has swept my little girl right off her feet." May spoke boldly.

Xan watched the two people she loved most in the world size each other up. Despite his lopsided smile, he submitted May to a long, searching glance before relieving them of their bags and putting them in the back of the pickup.

May, in turn, was taking in all six feet three of him as if she was trying to imagine his face without hair, his soul without its casing of tanned flesh, hard bones and whipcord muscle.

"I'm afraid the door is broken on the passenger side, ma'am." Opening the driver's door he said, "If you'll get in first and slide across, I'll take you and Xan to the motel in Wall where you'll both be staying tonight."

While May inched her way across the front seat and on to the catalogues, his eyes sent Xan a smoldering message. "It'll be hard spending the night on the ranch away from you. The only thing that keeps me going is knowing that after tomorrow, we'll be sleeping together as man and wife forever."

She loved his frank way of talking and wondered how she'd last until tomorrow night. But to be told something so intimate in front of May, and then to be kissed with such hunger, brought the heat to Xan's face. She finally found the strength to break their kiss and buried her face in his neck.

"Don't be embarrassed," he whispered, his hand lingering on the curve of her jeans-clad hip as he held her dangerously close. "She needs to see how it is with us. Right now I get the feeling she's not ready to let you walk down that aisle tomorrow."

"You're wrong," Xan murmured against the burnished column of his throat, trembling from their closeness. "My mother's wedding dress is in one of the bags. She would never have brought it if she didn't trust my judgment."

At her admission, his body tautened from emotion, letting her know he was the typical nervous bridegroom who wanted May's approval. She felt her heart expand with love for him.

"In that case I'd better take a little more money from my savings and get me some new clothes. I want to make you proud."

"I'm already proud of you, Judd. And you've already paid for that motel room for May and me tonight. Please don't spend any more money when you're trying to pay off your ranch loan," she urged quietly. "I know how hard you have to work and I don't care what you wear. Only our families will be at the church anyway, and the pastor won't think anything about it.

"In fact, if you'd rather I didn't wear my mother's dress, I won't. What's important is that May brought it to me. It's her way of giving us her blessing. She was once a farmer's wife and went through some very difficult times, so she understands. Don't you see that clothes don't matter?" she asked, gazing up at him with adoring blue eyes, silently begging him to listen to her.

Something flickered in the depths of his face before he crushed her against him so hard she could scarcely breathe. He hadn't said the words yet, but she knew in a secret part of her that he'd fallen in love with her. She wondered if a person could die from too much happiness.

Eventually he let her go. Feeling May's eagle eye on the two them, Xan climbed inside the cab, far too aware of his help because his hands seemed to cling to her hips before releasing her. Then he got in beside her and they left the airport, taking the freeway, headed for Wall.

If the lack of a window and air-conditioning bothered May, she never let it show. Though Xan was pleased that Judd and May conversed intelligently over the similarities and differences in ranching and farming, Xan had trouble concentrating. All she could think about was his thigh pressed against hers, the strong beat of his heart pounding in unison with her own.

Since the night Judd had gone outside to sleep in his truck, he'd put in even longer hours at the ranch and hadn't touched her. Not until today, in full view of May, had he succumbed to the needs building inside both of them, needs ready to burst out of control.

When they reached Wall, he drove directly to the motel and carried May's bags inside the room. Xan thought the three of them would go out for dinner, and was unbelievably disappointed when he announced that he had chores to finish at the ranch so he'd meet them tomorrow at the chapel, a little before two.

Xan told May she'd be right back, then followed Judd outside, hoping to change his mind about dinner. But he'd climbed in his truck and had shut the door before she could catch up to him.

The set of his firm jaw made her panic. "W-what's wrong, Judd? Have May or I said or done something to upset you?" she asked in a tremulous voice.

He stared at her with a brooding expression she'd never seen on his face before. "I thought you would have figured out the problem long before now."

Dear God. What if he had changed his mind?

Hot tears scalded her eyes and balanced on the brim of her black lashes. "A-are you regretting marrying me?" she asked with a bravery that was killing her. "I—I think May's presence has made all this too real to you."

Afraid to look into his eyes and see the truth, she lowered her head. "If you want to call off the wedding, please tell me before things go any further." The voice coming out of her was barely audible because her heart was broken, and he knew it.

After an ominous silence she heard him speak. "I guess there's still a whole lot we don't know about each other yet because the only problem bothering me right now is how I'm going to keep my hands off you until the ceremony."

His words had the effect of life-giving air after near suffocation. Her head flew back in reaction.

"Kissing you at the airport was a mistake," he confessed in a voice barely distinguishable from a growl. "If I stick around for dinner, I'll forget that promise I made to you and start our honeymoon tonight, May or no May."

With her heart in her eyes she admitted, "Tomorrow can't come soon enough for me, either."

"You shouldn't have said that. Now I won't be able to get to sleep tonight for dreaming about what you're going to look like in your mother's wedding dress."

A slight gasp escaped her throat. "Then you want me to wear it?"

"My brothers and I have a particular fondness for the picture of our mother in her wedding finery. It wouldn't seem right to cheat the children you and I are going to have out of the same privilege."

He had a way of saying things that lit up her life. But while they were on the subject, she decided to ask the question that had been consuming her. "Do you want a baby right away?"

Even from the distance separating them, his eyes seemed to glow an incandescent green. "Since I'm not getting any younger, I figure we better get started tomorrow night."

The pictures his words conjured up filled her body with a voluptuous warmth. "I'm so glad you said that. Though I didn't put it in the ad, I was hoping the man I chose to marry would want to start a family as soon as possible."

A hint of a smile broke the corners of his mouth. "Up until I met you, I shied away from the idea. But the night you hurt your ankle and I washed those pretty legs of yours in the tub, everything sort of changed, if you know what I mean."

Xan knew exactly what he meant. Heat suffused her face and she looked away.

"To be truthful, ma'am, keeping you pregnant will be no hardship."

Not for me, either, her heart whispered. She didn't even mind the fact that he kept calling her ma'am. Everything he said made her feel cherished.

But there was one thought that had occurred to her, one she felt they'd better discuss right now. "Judd? I hate to bring this up, but I think I'd better. What if for some medical reason I can't have a child?"

His gaze dropped to her flat stomach, and the playfulness disappeared. "Are you trying to tell me something?"

She sucked in her breath. "No. I'm just trying to anticipate any future problems. You deserve a wife who can give you children. Of course, I wouldn't hesitate to adopt. But if for some reason I can't conceive, I—I'll grant you a divorce, if that's what you want."

He flashed her an enigmatic glance. "I only plan on getting married once, so I guess we'll be adopting, if it comes to that."

"You mean it?" she cried.

"Since we're being honest," he replied in a strangely sober tone, "maybe now would be the time to tell you that if you marry me, the soddy will be your home for life. Naturally it won't be a hardship on me, not with you warming my bed every night. But most women want more...."

Xan wished she could tell him that despite her great wealth, material possessions had brought her no joy.

But the time wasn't right.

In fact, she was beginning to think it never would be right. Though she'd only known him a week, she was positive that if he learned about her background, he'd never believe she was willing to settle for what he would interpret as so little.

Biting her underlip nervously, she took a step closer to the truck. "I love the soddy, Judd. I plan to make it a real home for us."

Judd continued to stare at her, his eyelids lowered. He obviously *wanted* to believe her. But no thanks to his well-off brothers whose gibes must have done some serious damage, he was afraid.

Xan didn't suppose Judd feared anything in the world *except* her rejection of his life-style.

Since the only way to prove her words was to live there with him, she realized that winning his trust was going to take time.

For a moment she thought she saw a shadow of pain darken his eyes before he said, "Maybe May ought to see the ranch before you make any promises you can't keep."

Her instincts were right. Judd was worried, and it was up to her to reassure him before he called off the wedding.

He couldn't call off the wedding. If he did, her life wouldn't be worth living.

"May isn't marrying you. I am," Xan announced as if she was issuing a proclamation. "I came out here to find me a Bad man, and I found *you*. You're what I want, Judd Coltrain. If you're so unsure of me, then I'll live with you on your ranch until you're ready to marry me."

Now her voice was wobbling and her face was glowing red, but she couldn't help it. "A-and if you don't marry me, I'm not giving you a chance to marry anyone else because I plan on staying right by your side till I die," she almost shouted.

"If you don't show up for our wedding tomorrow, I'll come out to the ranch and find you. You might as well know right now that you'll never get rid of me.

"It doesn't matter what your brothers have said or done to make you feel so bad. I'm the only one who matters because—*because I'm the one who's in love with you!*"

She shouldn't have blurted it out that way. She should have waited to tell him when the time was right, but it appeared that time was running out.

"Would you mind saying that again?" he asked in a solemn voice, his expression unreadable.

Had she ruined it?

Finding it difficult to swallow, she said in a much quieter tone, "I'm in love with you."

A lifetime seemed to go by before he murmured, "Isn't it awfully soon to go making a rash statement like that?"

Maybe her instincts had been wrong. Maybe he hadn't fallen in love with her, after all. *Now she'd done it!*

Nodding jerkily, she whispered, "Yes. It is. But I can't help how I feel." She averted her eyes. "May thinks I was crazy to come out here in the first place to look for a husband. But the minute that dart landed in the Bad river, I felt as if destiny was calling to me. I *had* to come. I *had* to find out."

Judd's eyes were riveted to her mouth. "Run that by me again."

Xan knew what he was asking. It was truth time. "A-a lot of men have asked me to marry them."

"I can believe that," he muttered deep in his throat.

"But I could never say yes to any of them. Something always held me back. I decided I'd been going with the wrong kind of men because none of them were like John."

"John?" His dark brows knit together.

Was he jealous? She hoped so.

"Yes. May's husband. He was perfect. I made up my mind I wanted to find me someone exactly like him, but there aren't any men like that in New York. So that's when I came up with a plan to advertise for a husband."

Before she lost her nerve, she told him how May had tied the blindfold for her, how she'd thrown the dart with the result that she'd come to Wall.

His face became an expressionless mask. "So what you're telling me is, if that dart had landed in the Great Salt Lake, you'd have advertised for a husband in Utah and we would never have met."

How horrible that sounded.

"Yes. But since it landed in South Dakota, and we *did* meet, I know *now* that it was predestined. And *you* know it, too. Otherwise you would never have approached me in my booth, o-or invited me to have lunch with you at Pastor Swan's."

Warming to her subject, she persisted in the same vein. "In fact, you could have backed out at any time, but you didn't. Instead, you drove me to your ranch and said you'd show me a jackalope, which I still haven't seen, by the way.

"And after my accident, you told me you didn't want to drive me back to town. And then you kissed me, and that transformed my life for all time. So you see, even if you can't say the words I'm dying to hear, it doesn't matter because you're as crazy about me as I am about you. And all this talk about my not liking your ranch is pure nonsense. So I'll see you tomorrow, and you'd better be there,' she warned.

So saying, she stalked off toward her motel room, too wrought up to know exactly when he started up the motor and drove away.

CHAPTER SEVEN

"Has Judd arrived yet?" Xan cried out anxiously when May joined her in the small, carpeted reception room off the pastor's office. His wife had told Xan she could use it to change into her wedding gown. That was half an hour ago, and her watch indicated there were only fifteen minutes left until the ceremony.

"I didn't see his truck, but maybe his brothers brought him over when they came. If you want my opinion, not even a violent act of nature would prevent him from showing up to marry you. The way that man was kissing you yesterday made me blush, and I've never blushed in my life, so stop your fussing, lovey."

"Then you admit it's possible I'm not making a mistake."

May shook her head. "I didn't say that."

"Then you think it's only a physical attraction that will die out when the honeymoon is over," Xan murmured in pain because May still had her doubts.

"Not exactly." Her voice trailed off as loving eyes took inventory of Xan. "You're a heartbreaking beauty who could haunt a man like Judd Coltrain forever. When he sees you walking toward him in that simple white gown, he'll know he's the most blessed man alive." She started to choke up. "I just have to pray he'll always treat you the way you deserve to be treated. With love, and respect, and dignity."

"But that's the way he's been with me since we first met. Don't you see?" Xan pleaded with her.

"I'm afraid I've lived too long and have seen too much," May murmured. "You're a bright, loving spirit who has been the joy of my life. Promise me you won't let him change you." As she fit the Venetian-style cap on Xan's head, smoothing the veil, tears rolled down her cheeks.

"May!"

Mindless of the tailored satin dress with its prim collar and pearl buttons running from neck to hem, Xan threw her arms around the older woman and clung to her.

"Nothing's going to go wrong. I swear it. Now dry your tears, because I have some news that should ease your mind about the secret I've been keeping from Judd."

"What is it?"

"This morning, while you were in the shower, I phoned Mr. Raynor at his office. He has my power of attorney and I instructed him to draw up papers that relieve me of a terrible burden. Judd is now the sole possessor of the Harrington fortune, and he'll be able to do whatever he wants with it. After our honeymoon, he'll be notified."

"Roxanne Harrington! Have you taken leave of your senses? If he turns out to be no good, you'll have lost not only your heart, but your fortune!"

"May, you don't understand. The only way I could lose Judd would be to lie to him. But with one phone call I've fixed everything so that I can come to him as poor as a church mouse."

"And if he's the man you think he is, he'll erupt when he finds out you gave him your birthright for a wedding present!" May sounded scandalized.

"I plan to make him so happy on our honeymoon that when we get home and he hears the news, he'll know beyond any doubt how much I love him. Aren't you the one who taught me that love tames the savage beast?" she teased, trying to coax a smile from her beloved friend and mentor.

May was ashen faced. "Does he even have a clue how you happened to pick South Dakota for a hunting ground?"

"Yes," Xan answered honestly. "Before he left for the ranch last evening, I told him everything. So you see? Tonight I'll be able to face my new husband without any lies between us."

"I've told you all along you were playing with fire," May grumbled. "But after what you've just told me, I'm ten times as scared for you."

"You don't need to be."

Before May could say another word, there was a knock on the door.

Xan rushed over to open it. "Judd?"

"Sorry," both Judd's brothers said in unison.

"Can we talk to you for a minute?" Lon asked, sounding too solemn for Xan's peace of mind.

With her heart in her throat she said, "Is there something wrong? Where's Judd?"

"He's in the chapel with Pastor Swan," Kenny offered, sober faced.

"T-then I don't understand." her voice faltered. "Unless he's changed his mind."

"Changed his mind?" Lon sounded so shocked, it made her feel a little better.

Kenny heaved a deep sigh. "Look—we just came to warn you."

Not understanding any of this, she invited them in and intercepted a speaking glance from May. "Warn me about what?" she asked, closing the door.

"He showed up a few minutes ago in his overalls, said he was doing his chores until the last minute and didn't have time to get ready."

Xan smiled, wishing his brothers didn't care so much about appearances. "You don't need to worry about that. We already talked about what we'd wear. I love your brother. It makes no difference to me how he's dressed."

"But this is his wedding day," Lon muttered. "It isn't right. Mother would turn over in her grave."

"So would Dad," Kenny emphasized. "The thing is, we were asking him about where he was taking you for a honeymoon, and when he told us, we almost came to blows."

Her delicately arched brows met in a frown. "Why? What difference does it make to you if we hunt for fossils in the Badlands?" They always managed to find fault with him.

"The Badlands?" they cried at the same time.

"That's not where he's taking you," Lon muttered.

She blinked. "Then he probably wants to surprise me."

Kenny shook his head. "No woman would like the surprise he has planned for you. My wife would leave me if I pulled a stunt like that."

"Judd would kill us if he knew we were telling you about it, but you have a right to know. As far as we're concerned, you have grounds to back out of the marriage."

Indignant, Xan blurted, "I'll do no such thing! Where is he taking me?"

"He says he has his heart set on camping out on the Bad River for a couple of weeks. He muttered something about the place having special significance for the two of you."

"He said *that*?" Xan squealed for joy, her gaze capturing May's as if to say, "I told you so." But his brothers were too upset to hear the happiness in her voice.

Lon took her hand in a gentle grip. "Judd's not himself, Xan. What could he be thinking of, driving you out to that godforsaken place in a truck that might never make it back?"

"You don't know what it's like," Kenny inserted. "No one goes out there, particularly not a man who claims to love his wife."

Lon's grip tightened. "That's why we're here. To warn you before it's too late. You can slip out the back door of the church and we'll drive you to

Rapid City. Judd won't know anything about it until after you're gone."

"I don't know what happened to him," Kenny volunteered unhappily, "but ever since he met you, he's changed. We're sorry we ever showed him that ad because we don't think he's in any state to get married, and we'd feel responsible if he ever let you down."

Xan wanted to tell them that they'd noticed a change in his behavior because Judd had finally fallen in love, just as she had. The pastor had been the first to recognize the signs and had even teased Judd about it in front of her!

She wanted to tell Judd's brothers that they ought to be more supportive of him, especially after everything he'd done for them. But they were too agitated to listen to reason, so she said, "I appreciate your concern. I really do. But trust me, nothing you've told me has alarmed me in the least. He's the most wonderful man I've ever known and I'm going to marry him."

Lonnie's gaze fell away. "I just hope you won't live to regret it."

"Same here," Kenny murmured. "Even when he's normal, Judd's different from most men."

"I know. That's why I picked *him* for my husband."

"The thing is," Kenny explained, "if you decide you want to come home early from your honeymoon and Judd tries to talk you out of it, all you have to do is call us on the cellular phone and we'll send out a helicopter for you."

"We stashed it in one of the feed bags lying in the back of his pickup. Don't let him know it's there or he'll kill us. When he isn't looking, hide it in your things."

Xan didn't know whether to be touched or angered by their seeming concern for her welfare. She simply couldn't believe they were serious.

Was it possible they were having a hard time letting go of Judd? What was it he said the other night about them always following him around?

Maybe they were jealous of her place in his life. After all, when their father died, Judd had taken over the reins, becoming more than a big brother.

Even if some resentments remained—resentments Judd hadn't yet explained to her—perhaps the two younger brothers were feeling abandoned. Heaven knew Xan understood what that felt like. She'd lived with a grandfather who cared more about making money than he did about spending time with her.

Perhaps in the near future she could be the catalyst to unite the three brothers. Nothing could mean more to her than for all of them to become one big, happy family.

Just then the pastor's white-haired wife bustled in the room carrying a beautiful bouquet of pink roses and gardenias, which she thrust in Xan's arms.

"These are from your new family." She beamed.

"They're beautiful." Xan lifted it to her face to inhale the fragrance.

"So are you," both brothers whispered.

Xan started to choke up. "Thank you so much."

"I can hear the music. It's time," the pastor's wife broke in. "Lonnie, you're to join your brother and the pastor at the front of the chapel. Kenny, when the processional starts, you'll walk Xan down the aisle." She motioned to May. "Come along with me. Did I tell you my daughter drove down from Faith expressly to play the organ for Judd?"

But Xan was already feeling a tug on her heart. Before May disappeared, she rushed over to embrace the woman who would always mean the world to her. "Don't worry, May. I promise it will be all right."

"If you say so, lovey. God bless you," she murmured, bestowing a kiss on Xan's forehead before slipping out the door. That left Xan to follow with Kenny who, like Lonnie, looked handsome and elegant in a pastel summer suit and silk tie.

"You remind me a lot of Mother in that gown," he commented as he cupped her elbow and ushered her from the room. "When Judd sees you, he'll be sorry he didn't dress up."

Biting her tongue to control her temper she said, "Maybe one day when his mortgage is paid off, he'll be able to spend his money on a suit like yours."

"What did you say?" Kenny had stopped walking and was pulling on her arm.

Though she'd tried to sound nonjudgmental, Xan realized her comment had upset him, but now was not the time to get into it. "Can we talk about this later, Kenny? Listen—the processional has started. We have to hurry."

The second they reached the foyer leading into the chapel, her eyes fastened on Judd, who was listening to the pastor, Lonnie in place next to him.

Her relief at seeing that he'd come was so great, she didn't even notice his T-shirt and overalls. Flashing Kenny a brilliant smile, she laid her hand on top of his and started down the aisle of the beautiful little Gothic church with its exquisite stained-glass windows.

As if he had built-in radar, Judd's dark head lifted abruptly and their gazes locked. She felt an energy radiating from him that filled the near-empty chapel and made her heart pound so hard, she faltered mid-stride. If it hadn't been for Kenny's support, she might have fallen.

Though she hadn't met them yet, she knew that the two attractive blond women seated on the right were Kenny's and Lonnie's wives. On the left sat the pastor's wife and May, whose brown eyes were brimming with tears. As Xan drew near, she sent May a private smile, then met Judd's compelling stare once more.

He looked powerful as he stood there erect, that certain stillness he sometimes displayed in full evidence. Since her arrival in Wall, his unruly black hair with its tendency to curl had grown longer. She noted that his beard and mustache had started to fill in, reminding her more and more of a mountain man.

Tonight she'd have the right to love him in all the ways a wife could love a husband. The thought of it sent a thrill of excitement through her body.

She actually felt dizzy and clung to Kenny, who eyed her more than once with a worried expression.

The pastor motioned her forward with a smile, forcing her to let go of Kenny's arm. While Kenny took his place next to Lonnie, the pastor reached for Xan's free hand.

"Welcome to God's house, my dear. It's a holy thing you and Judd are about to embark upon. Here, Judd. Take her hand."

Xan felt Judd's warm hand close over hers in a solid grip, felt the force of his laserlike glance studying her profile until she could hardly breathe.

"That's fine." The pastor beamed exactly like his wife. "This is what I like to see. Two people who were meant for each other, joining hands and hearts in sacred matrimony.

"I didn't prepare a sermon because you've already written it, Xan. I have it in my pocket. It echoes what Judd has been saying ever since he was old enough to need a wife. I'm only sorry you didn't take it in your head to come out to South Dakota years ago. Poor Judd has had to wait a mighty long time for you." He winked at Xan. "But the waiting has come to an end.

"Now I want you two to turn and look at each other. Go ahead. Take a long look. That's right," he murmured as Xan lifted her gaze to Judd's. She could tell he was caught in the grip of some deep emotion because his eyes had gone a dark green, like the depths of a mysterious forest. She felt the force of it through his hand, which had tightened around hers, though she didn't think he was aware of it.

"Memorize each other. Twenty, thirty, forty, maybe fifty years from now, I want you to remember what it felt like to face your earthly companion with all the hope and joy and exultation you're experiencing right now."

Xan had already memorized Judd, every fascinating part of his mind and body. What she wanted was to burrow into his soul until they were joined together forever.

"Now repeat after me," the pastor began. "I, Roxanne Harrington, take you, Amasa Judd Coltrain, for my lawfully wedded husband, for better, for worse, for richer, for poorer, in sickness and in health, until death do us part."

Surprised that Judd had told the pastor her legal name, Xan almost forgot to say the words. In that slight hesitation Judd whispered, "It's not too late to back out."

Devastated by his words, she repeated the marriage lines louder than she'd intended, producing a chuckle from the pastor, who'd heard Judd's aside and obviously thought it funny.

"Now you, my boy. Repeat after me. I, Amasa Judd Coltrain, take you, Roxanne Harrington, to be my lawfully wedded wife, to have from this day forward, to love, to cherish, to watch over through sickness and in health, through hard times and good, as long as we both shall live."

Xan couldn't bear it if he backed out now and averted her eyes, afraid he might not repeat his part of the ceremony. But the pressure on her hand increased, forcing her gaze to Judd's.

"I, Amasa Judd Coltrain, take you, Roxanne Harrington, for my lawfully wedded wife. I vow to love, cherish and protect you in sickness and in health. I vow to never let you go, not in good times or the bad, especially not the bad," he said in a fierce tone she'd never heard come out of him before. It sent the oddest chill down her spine. "Only death will part us."

"Couldn't have said it any better myself," the pastor interjected. "And now, by the power invested in me by my holy office and the State of South Dakota, I pronounce you, Judd, and you, Roxanne, husband and wife. What God has joined together, let no man put asunder. Amen. Are you going to exchange rings?"

"No." Judd said it before Xan could.

"That's all right. It's a pagan ritual and has no spiritual significance. But kissing your bride is another matter altogether. Go on." He gestured to Judd. "I know this is the part you two have been waiting for."

Xan blushed scarlet and was a little nervous to express her feelings for Judd in front of May, who'd already witnessed their ardor the day before and had been shocked enough to comment on it.

Judd must have sensed her reluctance because he caught her around the waist and lowered his head till his mouth found hers. His kiss was long and hard, and it obviously pleased the pastor, who smiled in delight when Judd finally let her go.

She gasped for air and would have stumbled if Judd hadn't been supporting her with an arm around her shoulder, his fingers embedded deep in the satin so she could feel their heat.

"Would the congregation please rise?"

Dazed, Xan turned toward the pews, still leaning heavily against her new husband.

"I have the great honor to present Mr. and Mrs. Judd Coltrain. When they've reached the foyer, you guests may follow and congratulate them."

Moving in a trance, Xan walked down the aisle with Judd's arm wrapped around her waist, feeling the weight of his possession. Several times she buried her face in the flowers of her bouquet to hide her emotions. Judd's every touch signaled his impatience to get her alone, arousing her desire to a feverish pitch.

The next few minutes passed in a flurry of activity. Xan and Judd thanked the pastor and his wife, signed the marriage certificate, then greeted their families who pressed in on them and offered their good wishes. Xan felt particularly drawn to her new sisters-in-law. Both women were charming and expressed their disappointment that Judd wouldn't let them have a big party.

She would have liked to talk to them longer, but Judd suddenly announced that they were leaving and told Xan to hurry and change out of her wedding dress.

May followed her to the room off the pastor's office. Once the door was closed, they hugged and cried, then May started helping Xan out of her dress.

By the unnatural silence, Xan knew what the older woman was going to say before the words ever left her mouth.

"I've been to a lot of weddings in my time, but I never heard anyone change the vows like that before."

"He didn't change them, May," she said, stepping out of her dress to put on her Levi's. "He only emphasized certain parts to let me know that he'd never go back on his word."

"I'm not so sure about that. Lovey—don't let him take you away. Why don't you tell him you'd rather go back to the ranch."

"May!" Xan cried out in exasperation. "What are you afraid of?"

"I'm not sure. But something doesn't feel right. If you want to know the truth, I'm glad his brothers put that phone in the truck. Find it before Judd does and hide it in a safe place. I'm not going back to New York until you return from your honeymoon, so you can call me at the motel day or night."

Xan slipped on a cotton print blouse with an azure blue background and started buttoning it up. "I'm glad you're staying. You deserve a vacation. I heard the pastor's wife invite you over for dinner tonight. They're the kind of people who will involve you in everything. Please enjoy yourself and stop worrying about me."

A rap on the door brought her head around. "Mrs. Coltrain? Are you ready? We've got to get going if we expect to set up camp before dark."

Just the sound of his voice made her heart race. But for Judd to call her Mrs. Coltrain added another dimension to her happiness.

"I'll be right out, *Mr.* Coltrain."

"What's taking so long?" he asked.

May frowned. "That man's in too big of a hurry."

"And I suppose John wasn't?" Xan baited her as she applied a fresh coat of pink frosted lipstick.

"I'm leaving in one minute," he warned.

"Don't say it," Xan begged May. "Judd can't help it that he gets claustrophobic around his family. Maybe one day that will change, but now I've got to go. I'll come to the motel the second we get back. Take care of yourself and remember that I love you."

She threw her arms around May one more time, then ran from the room with her purse and overnight bag in hand. When she emerged from the church, Judd was already behind the wheel of the pick-up revving the engine. Apparently he'd done all the visiting he intended to do because his family was nowhere in sight.

Without saying a word, he got out of the truck and put her suitcase in the back, leaving her to climb inside the cab on her own. It surprised her that he didn't help her up, let alone touch her. Supposing that his mind was on the drive ahead of them, she decided it would be too sensitive and ridiculous of her to read anything else into it.

Though the afternoon heat was oppressive, it couldn't have been worse than the silence inside the cab. After they left the interstate outside Wall and headed east on Highway 14, Xan decided she couldn't stand it any longer.

"Are you going to tell me where we're going, or is it a surprise?"

His hands tightened on the wheel till his knuckles turned white. "It can hardly be a surprise to you since my brothers evidently warned you about going out to the Bad River with me."

She pushed a wayward black tendril out of her eyes, crushed that he'd learned of their meddling. "I'm sorry they involved me and made you angry. Let's forget about them and just enjoy ourselves."

"That's easier said than done. In case you decide to call for help, I'm letting you know now that I found the phone in one of the feed bags and tossed it in the trash."

Xan moaned, wishing with all her heart his brothers hadn't interfered. Their so-called good intentions were threatening to turn her honeymoon into a nightmare.

She shifted uneasily on the seat so she could look at him. "Judd? What happened between you and your brothers? I don't mean just today. Isn't it time you told me? I want to understand. When they upset you, it upsets me."

"Your loyalty is commendable, ma'am."

She sucked in her breath, as stung by his remark as by the use of that appellation, which made her feel distanced from him.

"Is it so hard to call me Xan?" she inquired gently.

His jaw tautened. "I guess some habits are difficult to break."

She lowered her head. "I'm not complaining. It doesn't really matter what name you use for me. It's how we feel about each other that counts."

"You're right about that."

His remark should have reassured her, but somehow it didn't. Evidently the problem with his brothers went layers deep, with a long history of pain, resentment and misunderstandings. He probably wished he was alone to deal with his black thoughts.

Not wanting to be a source of irritation, she turned away from him and rested her head against the back of the seat.

In truth, she was emotionally drained. Trying to calm May's fears—even *after* the ceremony—had taken its toll and had put another damper on her wedding day.

As her eyelids grew heavy, Xan came to the conclusion that she and Judd did much better when there was no interference from either side. She knew why he was taking her to the river and loved him for wanting to see the mythical spot where her dart had landed, the area that had drawn Xan to the prairie in the first place. She agreed that it was much the best idea.

If they'd gone to the Badlands, they would have had to deal with other people. How she longed to recapture the ecstasy of those first twenty-four hours with him, when no one had been around to spoil the magic.

Convinced that he was aching to be alone with her, too, she didn't mind that they'd turned onto a rut-filled dirt road, which couldn't have seen another car in days, or even weeks.

She was already drowsy from the strain and the heat, and the rocking motion of the truck threatened to put her to sleep. She hoped she wouldn't wake up until they'd arrived at their destination.

That's when she planned to become his wife in every sense of the word.

CHAPTER EIGHT

"COME on—it's time to help me make camp. Wake up."

Feeling the weight of Judd's hand on her shoulder, Xan forced her eyes open and lifted her head from its uncomfortable resting place against the corner of the truck.

When she could focus, she realized dusk had already settled over the badly eroded landscape. *She must have slept several hours!*

Praying the solitude had helped him work out his earlier frustration so they could start to enjoy their honeymoon, Xan darted him a covert glance. But the scowl on his face sent her spirits plummeting, and she was almost afraid to look in the direction of his fiery gaze.

Apparently the road didn't go any farther. He'd brought the truck to the edge of a gully ten or fifteen feet deep and about as wide. Even with his expertise she doubted he could have negotiated the long slope without them overturning. Maybe the latest four-wheel-drive Land Rover could have accomplished it.

Clearing her throat she asked, "How far are we from the river?"

"You're looking at it."

She blinked. *"This* is the Bad River?"

Naturally she'd heard about rivers that for one reason or another had dried up, or only filled during a spring runoff or some such thing, but she'd never seen one empty before.

The reality was so different from the image she'd carried in her mind since the day she'd thrown the dart, it took her a minute to adjust her thinking. Still, this spot was very precious to her.

She looked out the open window at the sky. "There's no storm threatening tonight." Drawing her head back, she turned to feast hungry eyes on her new husband. "Do you think it would be safe to sleep down there?" Flashing him a beguiling smile she said, "I'd like to see the look on May's face when I tell her we camped *in* the Bad River."

When he didn't say anything and only continued to stare at her with an unfathomable expression, she put a gentle hand on his arm. "What is it, Judd? Are you still so upset with your brothers?"

"You can cut the act now, ma'am."

For a moment, the silkiness of his tone deafened her to the cruelty of his remark. It was so unexpected, she felt sick to the pit of her stomach. *Something was wrong. Horribly wrong.*

"I don't understand," she said in a hurt whisper, still holding on to him.

"Don't worry about it. I have no doubts that come morning, you'll have figured it out."

Before she could comprehend it, he'd levered himself from the cab.

"Judd—"

She worked her way across the seat and jumped to the ground after him. But he moved with the swiftness of a prairie predator and climbed into the back of the truck.

As soon as he started lowering dilapidated gear over the side, she grabbed each item and set it in the wild grass. Devastated to see him like this, she cried, "You're just saying these hurtful things because you're in so much pain. But don't you know that nothing your brothers have said or done makes the slightest difference to me?"

He kept everything coming, but she had no idea if he was listening or not.

"I love being out here alone with you!" She practically shouted to get his attention. "Just the prairie and the stars and each other. This is *our* place, one I'll want to show our children some day. As far as I'm concerned, it's sacred—" her voice trembled "—because it brought me to you."

At that remark his dark head whipped around and he impaled her with eyes that showed no green at all.

"Judd—isn't it possible that your brothers are projecting their *own* wives' dislikes? But they have nothing to do with you and me. I thought you understood that."

Ignoring her attempts to communicate, he jumped down with a pitchfork in hand, walked a few yards off and started digging a pit.

"If you want to eat, you're going to have to make yourself useful," he muttered over his shoulder. "While I start a fire, you can get our dinner out

of there.'' He nodded to an old army-green duffel
bag. ''Somewhere around here is foil. Wrap each
buffalo steak with some potatoes and carrots in a
couple of sheets. Make them airtight.''

No matter how rude he was being, at least he was
talking to her. Convinced that part of his bad mood
could be remedied by a full stomach, she set about
her chores with a somewhat lighter spirit.

While he chopped an old log into firewood, she
organized everything and found the items she was
looking for. The vegetables must have come from
the root cellar.

''Do we have enough water to wash these off?''
she questioned, unable to keep herself from
watching the play of muscle across his shoulders
and back.

With unbelievable strength he sank the ax into
the last bit of log, splintering it into a dozen pieces,
then shot her a withering glance. ''If you're wanting
a bath later, then a little dirt in our food isn't going
to hurt us.''

Trying hard not to be wounded by his surly
manner, she only took enough water from the
thermos to clean the skins, then fixed their food as
he'd instructed. After meticulous preparation on
her part, she announced that their meal was ready
to be cooked. But if she had hopes that he would
thank her, or comment on her efforts, his next
words dashed them.

''We're going to need kindling. Bring me one of
those catalogues from the truck.''

Like an automaton, she walked over to the cab, reached inside and dragged one of them across the seat. Little did Sears, Roebuck and Company know how many uses Judd had found for their mail-order catalogue. There was even one in the outhouse. *For emergencies,* he'd told her when she'd mentioned it to him earlier in the week.

Had he actually ever ordered anything from them? she wondered as she carried it over to him and set it down at his feet. Judging by the sparseness of his furnishings, she doubted it. Despite her pain, she couldn't prevent a smile forming, one Judd wiped away with his words. "Start tearing it up."

Thankful for the encroaching darkness, which hid the beginnings of tears, she ripped out some pages, crushed them into wads and filled the pit.

Oblivious to her turmoil, he got down on his haunches to layer the kindling. The confidence and rapidity of his movements revealed that he'd done this many times before. Curious as it might be, she felt totally safe with him and would never consider camping out here with anyone else.

No matter how dreadful he was being right now, her heart forgave him because she knew he was battling something beyond his control, something soul-destroying. Before the night was over, she would use her love to ease his burden and give them the relief they both craved.

While he buried their dinner in the hot coals, she took hold of the old tarp and spread it on the grass for a ground sheet. There appeared to be only one bedroll. Two people could probably squeeze into it, but just barely. *Judd wouldn't be able to ignore her then,* she mused in satisfaction.

Once their bed was ready, she kept busy looking for plastic plates and the odd bits of cutlery he'd thrown in one of the drawstring bags. For dessert there were some apples. They could sit on the edge of the tarp to eat.

When she saw him pull the dinners from the fire, she filled their tin cups with water and put them next to the plates. Throughout the week she'd been here, Judd had served them nothing but buffalo meat, which a friend had given him.

The yellow fat was hard to get used to, but she liked the meat's flavor and texture well enough. Though she wouldn't want a steady diet of it, she didn't mind that they were having it again tonight. Especially when she opened the blackened foil and breathed in the wonderful aroma, reminding her how hungry she was.

"I think I like buffalo steak the best, especially when it's cooked like this," she offered, the only conversation of the last fifteen minutes as she swallowed her last bite of food. "My compliments to the chef. For a reward, enjoy one of my latest culinary triumphs while I do the dishes," she teased, handing him an apple before she stood up.

Because he was seated with his back to the coals, it was too dark to see his eyes, but she felt his body stiffen. Deflated because the food hadn't seemed to cheer him up, she kept herself busy washing things off and cleaning up every bit of mess.

When she'd run out of things to do, she took her overnight bag aside, found her toothbrush and wandered off a little ways to brush her teeth and get ready for bed.

Realizing that a filmy negligee wouldn't be appropriate, she slipped out of her clothes and put on her yellow knee-length velour robe with its three-quarter sleeves. Earlier that morning she'd applied perfume after her bath and decided she didn't need any more.

Judd liked things simple and natural, and tonight was too important to make any mistakes. There wasn't a woman alive who hadn't contemplated what her wedding night would be like long before the actual event. Since meeting Judd, Xan had run a constant fever just anticipating the moment he wrapped her in his arms.

The longing to be held by him propelled her back to camp in a hurry. But it appeared she'd have to wait because he'd wandered off. In a way, she was glad he wasn't there to witness her getting into his sleeping bag. It would be much better for him to come to her.

But one minute became five, then ten.

Alarmed, Xan sat up, listening for any sounds. "Judd?"

"I'm in the truck trying to get some sleep." His deep voice came out of the night air, which had started to cool in the last little while. "We won't be eating breakfast unless I find us a rabbit, and they're up before the sun."

She froze in place.

Whatever Judd's brothers had done, she wasn't about to let him brood over it any longer.

Quietly, she got up, gathered the sleeping bag under her arm and walked over to the truck. The proverbial saying about the mountain going to Mohammed didn't escape her as she climbed over the tailgate and slipped inside.

Judd had made a place for himself on the floor of the truck between all the paraphernalia, but the moment he saw her, he jackknifed into a sitting position, still fully dressed.

"What do you think you're doing?"

"Please don't let what happened at the church spoil our honeymoon," she pleaded with him, moving closer. "We were going to start a family tonight, remember?"

"There's no room in here."

Ignoring his off-putting remark, she stepped past him, put the bag down and sank to her knees. "What you need to do is unwind," she whispered near his ear, then gave the back of his neck a soft kiss before she slid her hands to his shoulders to massage them.

A tremor shook his powerful body and transmitted itself to hers. With a satisfied smile she found the rigid cords in his nape and slowly smoothed them. "You've worked far too hard since your father died, and there's been no one to take care of you. But now you have me, my darling."

Acting out of instinct, Xan moved her hands over his shoulders and across the front of his chest. She began kissing his hair-roughened jaw and cheek, aching to find his mouth. "Don't you know how much I love you?" Her voice trembled. "I'm the luckiest woman alive.

"To think that out of all the women who've wanted to belong to you, you married me. I know you're in love with me," she murmured feverishly, "even if you can't say the words. I—I don't need words, Judd. All I want is for you to hold me, to love me."

In the next breath, his hands grasped hers, bringing her caresses to an abrupt halt. "Unfortunately, it's not all I want." His voice grated.

There was a wealth of pain in those words. She knew what he was trying to say. He couldn't provide her with the luxuries of life. In taunting him about his plans to bring her out here for a honeymoon, his brothers had stripped him of his pride. It seemed that nothing she could say or do would repair the damage.

Unless...

"Judd," she whispered, rubbing her cheek gently against his. "I—I was going to wait until we'd returned from our honeymoon to give you your wedding present. But I've decided to tell you about it now because I can't bear to see you this upset."

His hands almost crushed hers before he let them go, leaving her bereft. "I wasn't counting on a wedding present, ma'am."

"I know. And before you admit that you don't have one for me, please hear me out." Her voice shook.

Encouraged when no comment was forth-
coming, she sat back on her heels and rested her
hands on his upper arms. "You haven't said anything about the relationship with your brothers, but
it's obvious there are serious problems. It's also
obvious that whatever their circumstances may be,
you've fallen on hard times.

"If you can't talk about it, then you can't. I won't
pry. But I *am* your wife and I want more than anything in the world to make you happy. My gift
should help."

"It would have to be some gift," he muttered
obliquely.

"A-actually, it is."

"You might as well know now that I don't set
store by such things."

She took a steadying breath. "I realize that. But
when we married, we agreed to share everything,
so it's not really a gift anymore."

"And what might that be?" His voice was
mocking, in what she knew was a front to cover
the wounds inflicted by family strife.

"T-the money my grandfather left me."

After a long silence, he asked, "Enough to buy
me a new truck?"

"Yes." She tried to sound unemotional and
folded her arms against her chest, so excited because he was listening to her, she was afraid to go
on touching him for fear she'd give everything away
too soon.

"Enough to buy a decent bed?"

"Yes, darling. Enough to buy you additional farming equipment and pay off your mortgage."

Watch what you're telling him, Xan. You're rushing him too hard.

"And you're saying that it's all mine, to use exactly the way I want," he drawled.

"Yes."

Judd shook his head. "I couldn't do that. I couldn't marry a woman for her money. Anyone who would marry another person for gain is worse than a snake whose belly slithers in the dirt," he said with such an intensity of distaste, Xan saw into the dark side of his nature and shivered.

"But you didn't marry me for my money," she said in a triumphant tone. "You didn't know I had any. The point is, it's not my money anymore. When we became man and wife, that money reverted to you. It's legally and lawfully yours, to do with as you please. You'll be getting the papers in the mail. I told the attorney to send them to you in care of general delivery in Wall."

Before she could countenance it, he'd gotten to his feet and had turned around, staring at her as if he'd never seen her before. Maybe the moonlight played a part, but she imagined that the mention of her gift was the true reason he'd paled beneath his burnished complexion, that his hands had balled into fists at his sides.

She'd never been so thankful for her inheritance as she was this minute. Judd's shock had robbed him of words, but she could hear his mind turning everything over.

Still kneeling at his feet, her face raised, she assured him, "I don't care how you use the money. If you want to put it all away for a rainy day, that's up to you. But if your brothers ever say or do anything to hurt you again in my hearing, they'll be sorry."

He stood there for an overly long moment, his eyes glittering with a strange light that almost frightened her. Maybe she shouldn't have said anything about his brothers. No matter what they'd done to him, they were his family. Besides, everyone knew that blood was thicker than water.

She would have apologized for her outburst, but he didn't give her a chance.

"You best stay in the truck where you'll be safe," he warned with a new violence, then vaulted over the side in a single bound.

Panicked because they hadn't talked everything out yet, she jumped to her feet and cried, "Where are you going, Judd?"

"I do my best thinking on my feet." As he walked away, the terse retort hung in the night air like a specter. She watched teary-eyed until he disappeared from sight, her heart heavy as stone.

When an hour had gone by and he still hadn't returned, she gave up her perch on the tailgate of the truck and lay down in the sleeping bag, which she'd stretched between the feed bags and generator.

Tossing and turning, she berated herself over and over again for having said anything derogatory about his brothers.

At best, family relationships were complicated. No one knew that better than she did. It was one thing to complain to Todd about her grandfather, but the second Todd commiserated with her about the older man's neglect, Xan was always the first one to get upset and then come to her grandfather's defense.

It didn't make sense, but human emotions rarely did. In that regard, Judd was no different. Out of a desire to show him how much she loved him, she'd offended him and needed to tell him she was sorry.

Throughout the endless night she heard the occasional cry of what Judd had told her a few evenings ago was a coyote. But it was guilt, not fear that prevented her from closing her eyes. If she was alone on her wedding night, she had no one to blame but herself. She should have been more patient with Judd.

Xan hadn't realized how sensitive he was on the subject of his family, and she made up her mind she'd never push him again about anything. He was the kind of man who had to come to decisions on his own, especially where his brothers were concerned.

She would honor his privacy and was anxious to tell him as much. But she had a long wait. She didn't hear his footsteps until the first pink-tinged fingers of dawn splayed like a fan across the sky.

"Good. You're up," he muttered the second he saw her slip over the end of the tailgate and walk toward him.

"I—I'm glad you're back," she stammered, afraid she looked a sight after her sleepless night. "Judd, forgive me for saying anything about your brothers. I had no right, and I promise it will never happen again."

"You're right about that." He made the cryptic remark as he started loading the back of the truck with their gear.

Xan didn't understand. "I thought you were going to go rabbit hunting for our breakfast."

"I've changed my mind. We're heading for home."

"Because of what I said?" she half-moaned the question. "Don't let that ruin our honeymoon. Can't we start over and pretend we've just arrived? I'll hunt with you."

His answer was to drop her overnight bag at her feet. Storm-green eyes swept over her robe-clad figure with a slow, intimate, insulting scrutiny she'd seen in the unflattering perusal of other men, but never from him. It turned the husband she adored into an enigmatic stranger.

"Get dressed!"

His brutal dictate made her gasp. She shook her head disbelievingly. "What's wrong? Why are you being like this? I've apologized about your brothers, so I assume you're upset about my wedding gift to you. But how could you be? When I advertised for a Bad man, I said that I expected to share everything with my husband. We're partners now. What I have is yours, what you have is mine."

The glint of fury in his eyes was like a physical blow, wiping away all the magic of the last seven days as if it had never been. In its place, the warnings she'd ignored came screaming back at her.

Even when Judd's normal, he'd not like other men.

Sometimes things change after you say "I do." You're playing with fire and you're going to get hurt.

There's something wrong with a man who has remained a bachelor so many years all of a sudden wanting to get married this fast.

There are worse things than being wanted for your money. At least with Todd, you wouldn't experience many unpleasant surprises.

I don't know what happened, but ever since he met you, he's changed.

As far as we're concerned, you have grounds to back out of the marriage.

We're sorry we ever showed him that ad because we don't think he's in any state to get married, and we'd feel responsible if he ever let you down.

We're here to warn you before it's too late.

Something doesn't feel right, lovey. I've been to a lot of weddings in my time, but I never heard anyone change the vows like that before.

I, Amasa Judd Coltrain, take you, Roxanne Harrington, for my lawfully wedded wife. I vow to never let you go, not in good times or the bad, especially not the bad. Only death will part us.

Xan started to shake and couldn't stop. *Had her desire to find a husband who didn't know she was*

*an heiress blinded her to everything else? Had her
instincts let her down?*

She couldn't believe it. How could anything that
had felt so right as marrying Judd be so wrong?
Even the pastor had told her theirs was a marriage
made in heaven. But on the heels of that thought
came another of May's warnings.

*Not even the pastor knows what goes on behind
locked doors. Once you're alone with this man, he
might turn out to be someone quite different.*

"I'm ready to pull out." The rough, surly voice
broke in on her tortured thoughts, devastating her.
"Get in the truck."

"I'm not dressed yet," she answered in a dull
tone.

"That's too bad. We're leaving."

In the next instant he reached for her, sweeping
her into his arms in an iron grip before depositing
her on the front seat of the cab, displaying none of
his earlier concern or gallantry.

Too wounded for tears, Xan edged her way across
the seat to the catalogues, unaware, until it was too
late, that his callous treatment had popped the
bottom buttons of her robe, causing the material
to part at the hem. Nothing escaped his all-seeing
eyes, certainly not the sight of one long, slender
leg, bared from sandal to creamy thigh.

Humiliated, she clutched the velour material to
cover herself, but not before his icy stare did its
damage. She'd barely had time to make herself
decent before he'd tossed her overnight bag in the

back of the truck and had levered himself into the cab behind the wheel.

The silent drive to the highway was the longest, blackest, most excruciatingly painful time of her life. Though her tailored robe looked perfectly proper, she couldn't believe he was capable of humiliating her like this.

Whatever demons drove him, his abject cruelty had robbed her of all desire to fight them. His brothers had warned her he wasn't normal, but she hadn't listened to anything except her own foolish heart. Now she had the devil to pay, as May was fond of saying.

May.

Thank heaven she was still in South Dakota, waiting for Xan to get back from her honeymoon. Xan had never needed the older woman more than she did at this moment.

"J-just drive me into Wall and leave me at the motel. Then you can go back to the ranch and we never have to see each other again."

The only indication that he'd heard her was to gun the motor as they drove past the turnoff for his ranch. It was what she wanted, but her heart broke a second time as the truck ate up the miles, separating her from a place where she'd known the greatest happiness of her life.

Unfortunately it was an ephemeral happiness that couldn't last. Judd hadn't even made love to her yet. Now he never would. . . .

Xan clung to the truck door, grieving for the man she had thought him to be. The Bad man of her dreams. But that's all he was. A dream—with no substance.

She prayed the sign for Wall would appear soon. The hostile tension radiating from the man at her side made their close proximity unbearable. It didn't help that at seven in the morning, the vacation traffic was already heavy on the road, slowing things down.

Finally, when she thought she might jump right out of her skin, she spied the turnoff in the distance that would bring her to the end of a torturous journey.

Desolation swept over her as she imagined the empty years ahead. No man could ever match the Judd her heart had embraced.

Another voice buried in her psyche promised that no man would ever again be given the chance to turn her dreams into nightmares.

So deep was her turmoil, it took her a second to realize that Judd hadn't followed the other cars off the highway. Experiencing the awful premonition that he'd purposely missed the turnoff, she jerked her head around, her heart hammering with an unnamed dread.

"Judd?" Her voice caught. "What's going on? Why didn't you drive into Wall?"

"Because I'm taking you home."

She lowered her head, fighting tears. "May and I will make our own arrangements to get back to New York. Please turn around and let me out at the motel. You couldn't possibly want to continue this farce any longer."

"What I want has nothing to do with it, ma'am,"
he drawled with heavy sarcasm. "Until death do
us part. That's what the pastor said, and that's the
way things are going to stay."

CHAPTER NINE

THE closer they drew to Rapid City, the more appalled Xan grew. *Would he actually drop her off in front of the terminal while she still wore her bathrobe?*

On the point of being physically sick to her stomach, she contemplated jumping out of the truck at the next stop light and taking her chances that a stranger would help her. But the door couldn't be opened, so unless she slipped through the broken window, there was no hope of escape from her side.

"Don't even think about it," he muttered, displaying a frightening clairvoyance.

Inwardly shrinking from the stranger he'd become, Xan avoided his withering gaze by staring out her window. Suddenly it didn't matter that she wasn't dressed to be seen in public. All she cared about was getting away from his inexplicable anger.

When he drove past the turnoff for the airport and followed the signs leading to Mount Rushmore in the Black Hills, her panic escalated.

She'd always wanted to see the famous monument of four presidents whose faces had been carved from the granite mountains. But not under these circumstances.

"Whatever awful thing you imagine I've done to you, it doesn't warrant this kind of behavior. Let me out of the truck, Judd."

"You're my wife," he taunted in a lethal tone, tearing her apart. "Yesterday I promised before God to protect and watch over you. That's what I intend to do."

"Yesterday I thought you loved me," she said in an agonized whisper. "Now I know differently. If you have any compassion in you, please don't carry this any farther."

But her impassioned plea fell on deaf ears, and she wondered if he intended to drag her up on top of the monument and fling her to the depths.

Normally the sylvan beauty of the famed wooded mountains would have delighted her and made her want to get out and explore the nature trails and caves with Judd. But right now her pain over the drastic change in him overshadowed everything else.

What made it so much worse was the fact that part of her was still aware of the physical attraction he held for her. No matter how he treated her, she couldn't reverse the chemistry that drew her to him, that made her yearn to feel his arms around her.

How could she still entertain these kinds of thoughts when he'd been deliberately cruel and hurtful to her since the ceremony yesterday? It didn't make sense.

A sharp turn to the left forced her to brace herself so she wouldn't fall against him. Now they were headed away from Mount Rushmore, and she couldn't begin to second-guess his intentions. Soon they had passed through Hill City. She had no choice but to hang on as the truck began another serpentine ascent.

The grandeur of the mountains seemed a bitter irony when the atmosphere in the cab was so explosive that the slightest spark could set off a dreaded conflagration.

She closed her eyes to prevent tears from forming, not opening them again until the truck suddenly swerved to the right, its tires making the kind of screeching sounds that invariably preceded a bad accident.

Anticipating the crash, her lids flew open almost too late to read the sign for the Lazy L Ranch. Relieved to discover that the private road held no other cars, she should have been reassured. But in point of fact, her fear increased because it looked like Judd had decided to pay his brothers a visit.

When there was so much wrong between her and her husband, she couldn't imagine anything worse than a family confrontation with the wives witness to his rage.

As if to protect herself from additional grief, Xan shrank against the corner of the seat, dreading his next move. But even in her agonized state, she couldn't prevent the gasp that escaped when she first caught sight of the majestic ranch house set among the pines. Lush-green mountains with a canopy of hot blue sky provided a fairy-tale backdrop.

Except for the western A-shaped design and hand-hewn logs caulked with oakum, she felt she was looking at a king's palace tucked away in the Vienna Woods of Austria.

The ultimate hunting lodge for a sovereign and his courtiers.

Xan no longer wondered why Judd's fabulously wealthy brothers looked down on his tiny prairie soddy with such disdain. Both Ken and Lonnie's families would be swallowed up inside such a mammoth edifice, which rivaled her grandfather's New York mansion bordering Central Park.

Another pain pierced her heart, one more intense than she'd ever known before because Judd wouldn't allow her close enough to help protect him from additional hurt.

In the parking area to the right she saw several four-wheel drives bearing the Lazy L brand, the kind of vehicles his brothers had been driving when they'd first met Xan at Judd's soddy.

She'd been praying that they wouldn't be home, but until this moment she'd forgotten that it was a Sunday morning, probably the one time during the week they could all sleep in and be with their families.

But there would be no peace or enjoyment when Judd burst in on them, dragging his wife of twenty hours with him. Judging by the tautness of his body as he flung open the door and levered himself from the cab, he intended doing just that.

With a merciless glint in his eyes, he reached across the seat and grabbed hold of her wrist. "Don't shrink from me now, beloved," he baited, tightening his grip.

Powerless against such aggression, Xan was pulled to his side where he picked her up in his arms and started for the ranch entrance.

She couldn't bear it. "Put me down!" she begged, fighting him in earnest, but it was like trying to struggle out of a straitjacket. "Don't do this, Judd. Please." Her voice caught. Up until now she'd managed to suppress her tears, but the closeness of their bodies penetrated her defenses and the dam burst, wetting her cheeks until they glistened.

A chilling smile broke the contours of his mouth. "Tears, my darling? Isn't it every bride's dream to be carried over the threshold? Especially this one?" he whispered in a menacing tone. "I'm only doing what you've had your avaricious little heart set on ever since you were old enough to vamp every rich boy on the block."

Physically and emotionally drained, it took a moment for his words to affect her. By then, he'd carried her through the front doors, and an unfamiliar female voice called out, "Judd! We all thought you were on your honeymoon. What's wrong with Mrs. Coltrain?"

"Nothing that a day in bed won't fix, Iris," he assured her in a mocking voice. His comment could only be taken one way. Humiliated, Xan's face turned crimson, a reaction he noted with sardonic pleasure. "I'll let you know when we need food."

Before Xan could take another breath, his mouth descended, seizing hers in a merciless kiss, as if he meant to devour her. All the way up the rustic staircase and down a hallway of one wing he carried her like a spoil of war, his kiss a grinding, punishing travesty of the physical affection he'd shown her earlier in the week.

She didn't realize they'd entered a bedroom until he suddenly tore his lips from hers and tossed her into the middle of a king-size bed.

"Welcome home, Mrs. Coltrain." He bit out the words with a sneer, his eyes a turbulent green as they roved over her bare limbs with unconcealed distaste.

In a state of shock, Xan scrambled to her knees, trying desperately to keep the robe from separating. "W-what do you mean, *home*? This is your *brothers'* home!"

His livid expression terrified her. "Like all liars, you've started to believe your own fabrications."

"*What* fabrications?' Xan cried out, wondering if she was in the middle of a ghastly nightmare. She didn't have the faintest idea what he was talking about, but somewhere deep inside she had the awful premonition that he believed everything he was saying.

"Did you honestly think you could get away with it?" he lashed out, incapable of concealing his rage.

Bewildered, she could only shake her head. "Get away with *what*? I thought you'd had a serious falling out with your brothers, that you were a down-and-out rancher, that the soddy was your home, not the Lazy L."

Praying he'd deny it, that he'd end this hell and take her in his arms, Xan slid off the bed in order to face him, her hand unconsciously holding the edges of the lace-trimmed collar together. But a horrifying silence stretched between them, and she felt something deep inside shrivel up and die.

Like the bits of colored glass in a kaleidoscope, which formed a whole new pattern with one twist of the cylinder, fragments of knowledge started coming together to present her with a whole new picture of Judd, one she could scarcely assimilate.

"You were living a lie the night you approached me at my booth," she whispered in agony. "I can't believe it. Not you," she moaned, feeling the blood drain out of her face.

She thought she saw a shadow of pain in the recesses of his eyes. But his mouth suddenly tightened, dispelling that small hope.

"I have to hand it to you, Mrs. Coltrain. You're good. With that husky little catch in your voice, and those violet eyes that go all dewy on cue, you're so damn good, you could bring any man to his knees and make him a beggar for life. Any man, that is, *except* me."

He started for the door.

Delayed shock prevented her from going after him until he'd disappeared from the room.

"Wait!" she cried out, running down the hall behind him, but he'd already reached the stairs. "You've got everything wrong. Please. Let me explain. I'm not who you think I am."

Pausing on the landing, his hands balled into fists, he muttered, "That's the first honest thing to come out of your mouth since we met."

Gone was any trace of his charming drawl, the one that had tugged at her senses that first night of the rodeo. In its place were the acid tones of a sophisticated man who was used to being in charge and obeyed.

His eyes held a frightening glitter. "My brothers had no idea they were up against a real pro. It *almost* excuses them."

"Judd, your brothers have nothing to do with you and me. Until they came to your ranch that day, I swear I'd never seen them before in my life!"

Everything she said seemed to infuriate him more. With sinking heart she realized there was no reaching him.

Crazed with pain and the fear that he would disappear, she said, "Whatever it is you imagine your brothers and I have done, I don't recall anyone forcing you to marry me."

"That's right," he said in a sinister tone. "I decided to let you have what you deserve because it fit in with *my* plans."

"*What* plans?"

"Now that I'm a married man, my brothers will get the hell out of my personal life and stay out! As for you, you can enjoy my considerable wealth for as long as we both shall live. You'll never want for anything."

"Stop it, Judd!" She almost screamed the words. "You don't know what you're saying! Your money is the last thing I need or want, and I can prove it. Just hear me out!"

"Sorry, ma'am. I can't spare the time. My men are waiting for me to join them on a cattle drive. This is your home now. Any woman who would go to the lengths you did to marry the wealthiest man in the state of South Dakota deserves some sort of reward." His words dripped with a soul-deep bitterness.

You're wrong, Judd, her heart whispered. *So wrong... What an irony that in marrying me, you're vastly more wealthy than you were before.*

He flashed her a venomous glance. "Enjoy my money to your heart's content. But let's get a few things straight. We were married by a man of God, which means you will remain my wife—even when you grow bored with your role as Mrs. Coltrain and want to run after your next victim. Should the day come that I find out you're pregnant, you and I and God will know it's not my child. That's the day your funds will be cut off."

By now he was almost out of sight. "Judd—you can't go like this!" she shouted at him, uncaring that his staff could hear them. "I can prove you're completely wrong about me, that everything I've been telling you is God's truth."

"*God's* truth?" He threw back his head, his eyes dark as flint. "How dare you use His name after what you've done."

If she hadn't been telling the truth, his chilling words would have demoralized her.

"As God is my witness, I came out to South Dakota exactly as I told you, to find a husband." Swallowing hard she said, "What I didn't tell you is that I came to find a husband who wanted *me*, not my money."

"*Your* money?" he asked caustically.

"Yes, the fortune my grandfather left me."

With the distance separating them, she couldn't tell if his ashen color was a mere trick of light.

"Lady, with your looks and acting ability, I don't know why you're not in Hollywood making your *own* fortune."

In the next instant, he was gone.

Xan flew down the staircase and raced after him, but by the time she opened the massive front door, he'd already started up one of the estate vehicles and was barreling down the drive.

Acting on pure instinct, she flew to his battered truck and climbed in the cab, determined to catch up with him. It no longer mattered that she was still dressed in her robe.

Judd had to be stopped and made to listen to her!

Thankfully, the keys were still in the ignition and the motor turned over without problem.

Out of the corner of her eye she saw Iris standing in the doorway, a look of incredulity on her face. Xan didn't have time to stop and explain. Without a second to lose, she pressed on the gas and shifted gears, wishing the old truck had wings and could fly.

To her dismay, the twists and turns of the private road, combined with the heavy foliage, prevented her from glimpsing the Blazer. When she reached the mountain road, she had no idea which way he'd turned, but could only assume he'd headed toward Rapid City. All roads led from there to the far-reaching areas of the state.

Unfortunately, his cattle ranch could be anywhere. The longer she drove without seeing a sign of him, the more she realized the futility of trying to catch up to him, especially in her state of undress.

Swallowing her sobs, she did the next best thing and headed for Wall, needing May more than she'd ever needed anyone in her life.

Xan wasn't nearly as afraid of May's reaction as she was of Judd's need for revenge against her and his brothers.

What had jaded him to such an extreme that he would go as far as marriage to inflict this kind of punishment when she knew he had feelings for her? *Or did he?*

Was he acting the entire time? Could a man fake the kind of kisses he'd given her, the kind of emotion that had made their bodies tremble in passion whenever they got near each other, let alone held each other? Could a man's eyes change color at will?

Before the day was out, she prayed to have answers from Ken and Lonnie. She mentally prepared what she'd say to them as she left the highway and entered Wall.

Because it was late morning, the parking lot outside the motel had emptied of cars. Relieved that no one would notice her in her bathrobe, she jumped from the cab and climbed in the back of the truck to find her purse and suitcase.

"May?" she called out a minute later, knocking on the motel room door, tears streaming down her cheeks. When there was no answer, she reached in her handbag for the spare key to gain entrance and almost collided with her housekeeper, who let out a shocked cry and dropped the toothbrush she was holding.

"Lovey, what's wrong? What are you doing back this soon dressed like *that*?"

"Oh, May." Xan moaned in pain. "Thank heavens you're here."

When she felt the older woman's arms go around her, she broke down in heart-wrenching sobs and poured out her heart to the one person who in the past had always been able to make everything better.

But not this time, her heart warned her. *Judd* was the only person who could make her world right again, and he was gone, inaccessible—perhaps forever.

May never once said I told you so. All she did was listen, and when Xan finished describing everything that had happened since the wedding ceremony, May agreed Xan should contact Judd's brothers and set up a meeting.

"They gave you that cellular phone for a reason, lovey. It's time you found out the truth about the man you married, and they're as good a place to start as any!"

Without wasting a second, Xan placed a call to the Lazy L, asking Iris to contact Lon and Ken and tell them to phone her at the motel right away.

Since it might be a while before they heard anything, May listened for the phone so Xan could shower and get dressed. When that was accomplished and there was still no word, May offered to go out and get them some lunch from a fast-food restaurant around the corner. Though Xan protested that she couldn't eat anything, May ignored her and said she'd be right back.

While she was gone, the phone rang. To Xan's relief, Lonnie was on the other end. He assumed she needed help and couldn't figure out why she hadn't called earlier on the cellular phone.

Needing to be discreet, Xan simply explained that Judd had been called away on a cattle drive, which provided her the perfect opportunity to meet Judd's brothers on a matter of some importance. She asked him to contact Ken and come to the motel lobby in Wall as soon as possible.

Lon said they'd take the helicopter and meet Xan at the Silver Corral Café directly across the street from Wall Drug, at three. The place would be more private and intimate so they could talk.

Three o'clock couldn't come soon enough for Xan. Unable to stand her own tortured thoughts, she replaced the receiver and hurried outside to join May. After they ate, they could go window shopping in the heart of town—anything to get through the next few hours until Xan had an explanation for the pain her brand-new husband had relished inflicting on her.

On the dot of three, Lon and Ken walked through the café doors, immediately spying Xan and May who'd found a booth in the corner where the four of them could talk.

Once they were seated and orders had been taken, Xan stared at one brother, then the other, wondering how much to say, how much to give away and still remain loyal to her husband.

After several aborted attempts, she said, "You warned me not to marry Judd, so it's obviously come as no surprise that everything has fallen apart. You were right about your brother." Her voice shook. "When he went through with that farce of a wedding ceremony yesterday, he had revenge in mind because he believed I had married him for his money."

Silence fell around them like mist.

"We figured money had something to do with the reason he was acting so strange," Lon finally murmured, his expression bleak.

Ken's worried countenance mirrored Lon's. "Please tell us you didn't marry him because of that." His hurt voice tugged at her heart, and it came like a revelation that they both loved and adored their older brother.

"I can set your minds at rest on that point," May inserted in a no-nonsense tone, causing their heads to turn. "You've ranched all your lives. My guess is, you own a lot of equipment with the Harrington brand."

Both of them looked puzzled, but they nodded.

"About two years ago there was an article in *Forbes* about the owner and founder of the

Harrington Corporation. Did either of you happen to read it?''

They shook their heads, but Lon said, ''I remember Judd saying something about the founder being an engineering genius, that he'd become one of the wealthiest men in the United States.''

''You're partially right,'' May interjected. ''I was his personal housekeeper until his death last year when the newspaper listed him as the wealthiest man in North America. Now his granddaughter, Roxanne, his only living kin, has the distinction of being the wealthiest woman.''

''Did have,'' Xan cautioned May.

Comprehension dawned. Xan could have laughed when she saw the look of incredulity that broke out on her brothers-in-law's faces. Taking advantage of their speechless state, Xan added, ''Judd's very old-fashioned, and I was afraid he wouldn't marry me if he knew I was an heiress. You see—'' her voice caught ''—I believed he was a dirt-poor rancher who had nothing more going for him than sheer grit and the determination to succeed. So yesterday morning, I instructed my attorney to turn over my entire fortune to Judd, a sort of wedding present. I told Judd I was giving him the inheritance from my grandfather, but h-he has no idea of the amount. The papers won't come for a couple of weeks. But that's only one of my concerns.''

Her gaze darted from one to the other. ''Before he stormed out of the ranch house this morning, he said some pretty ugly things that only you two might be able to explain.''

By the way they averted their eyes, her comment didn't seem to sit well with them. Mystified, she asked, "Would you please tell me what he meant when he said, 'My brothers had no idea they were up against such a pro. It almost excuses them.'"

Again, silence reigned until Ken patted Lon's arm. "Go on. You tell her."

Clearing his throat several times, Lon finally said, "Ken and I have always felt bad that Judd had to work so hard to keep everything going after Dad died. He continually sacrificed his own wants and needs to help Mom and us.

"The thing is, he does the work of a dozen men and never knows when to quit. It makes us feel guilty as sin for living our lives like normal people. We figured that if he got married, he'd have to slow down a little bit and take life easier. But he's always said he doesn't have time for women, which is ridiculous because they throw themselves at him, lie in wait for him, make themselves available day and night. Hell, he could have gotten married a hundred times over, and that's no lie."

"He's telling the truth," Ken corroborated. "For the last few years, Lon and I have tried to help some of the women who really cared for Judd by setting things up for them. You know, aiding and abetting nature so that he'd be forced to take a second look and fall for one of them."

"Unfortunately, our last ploy blew up in our faces and Judd didn't speak to us for six months," Lon lamented. "We wouldn't want to live through that again, so we swore off matchmaking for good."

Xan was beginning to read between the lines. "Then how do you account for the fact that you showed him my advertisement in the *Bison Courier*?"

"We didn't!" they asserted in unison.

Taking a sharp breath, Xan said, "Judd told me it was because of you two that he saw the article in the first place."

"No." They shook their heads and Ken said, "Judd takes several newspapers, including the local papers. Your ad ran all month in all of them. He must have seen it every time he turned around. On one of his visits to Meadow to bawl us out for something we'd done wrong, he mentioned the article and we told him we'd seen it, too."

"Yeah," Lon chimed in. "I told him it reminded me of our mother, the kinds of values she used to implant in us. The thing is, we all loved Mother, but I'm pretty sure Judd put her on a pedestal. Maybe that's the reason he's never married, because no other woman has been good enough."

Ken nodded solemnly and eyed Xan. "Until *you* came along."

"Maybe he thought you two collaborated with me to set up that ad." Xan shivered as she said it.

The two brothers looked at each other. "It's possible."

"It's not only possible, it's the answer," Lon exclaimed. "Because of the special wording in that ad, Judd assumed we were in league with Xan, trying to get to him through the subtle reference to Mother. He thought Xan was a fortune hunter and decided to pay each of us out. No wonder he bought that old truck and told everyone he had business at the soddy. All this time he's been planning his revenge. It's scary.''

"Scary doesn't begin to describe it." Xan moaned, remembering every calculated step of his whirlwind courtship, which he'd been orchestrating from the beginning.

She never saw it coming.

Ken put a hand on her arm. "Please don't get me wrong, Xan. You're the most beautiful woman I ever laid eyes on, and Judd would have to be blind not to agree. But if he was that angry with you, do you have a clue why he went through with the ceremony?"

"No," she whispered. "After he took me to the Lazy L this morning, he said that marrying me would get you two off his back. He also said that I could spend his money any way I wanted, but if I had any idea of leaving him, I could forget it. We were married by a man of God and we would stay married until the bitter end. He also said that if I got pregnant, he and I and God would know that it wasn't his child. That would be the day he'd cut off my funds." Her voice trembled. "Then he walked out."

CHAPTER TEN

"ANY man who would do that to a woman, let alone my lovey, doesn't deserve to breathe the same air she does," May proclaimed and rose to her feet.

Lon and Ken followed suit, their expressions anxious. "Don't do anything yet," Lon pleaded. "This has all been a huge misunderstanding."

Ken put a hand on her arm. "We're going to go after Judd and make him listen to reason. When he knows the truth, he'll be back to straighten things out."

"He'll be too late," May interjected coldly. "Judd Coltrain isn't fit to be anyone's husband. Come on, Xan. We've got to make reservations to fly home to New York. When Mr. Raynor hears the truth, he'll have that marriage annulled so fast, your erstwhile husband won't have time to blink."

Xan got up from the table in an emotional daze, too drained and hurt to think. Her mind kept going over those special moments with Judd. It didn't seem possible that he'd been playing a part every step of the way, even to repeating false vows in front of Pastor Swan.

But it appeared she'd been lied to and used. She had to accept the fact that Judd didn't love her, that the raw hunger she had sometimes seen in his eyes had all been make-believe.

171

As May ushered her out of the restaurant to the truck, Xan promised Judd's brothers that she'd stay in touch with them. Beyond that, everything else was a blur.

By the time they'd arrived at their room, she was heaving great sobs and couldn't seem to stop. While May dealt with the packing and checked them out of the motel, she told Xan to have a good long cry.

In less than an hour, they were on their way to Rapid City with May at the wheel. They would spend the night at a motel near the airport, then be up early for their morning flight to New York.

Xan couldn't believe it was ending like this. It felt like she was on her way to the death chamber. She didn't argue with May, who took charge of her and made all the necessary arrangements. Nothing mattered. She feared nothing ever would again.

The night seemed endless. Xan suffered torture at the thought of never seeing Judd again and stifled her groans in the pillow, soaking it with her tears. Just thinking about the two of them at the soddy gave her heart a great leap.

If he ever did hear the truth and finally believed it, would he want their marriage annulled so they could both be free to pursue their individual lives? Or would he want them to stay married and explore what might be between them?

Those questions kept her tossing and turning until first light. By morning she knew what she had to do, and when she and May drove to the airport to park the truck, Xan announced that she wasn't going to go to New York.

"I can't leave like this, May. I love Judd. Someday he's going to know the truth. When that happens, I want to be here in case there's a marriage to salvage."

May must have known it would be pointless to try to persuade her differently because she said, "I was afraid you'd insist on staying. Where will you go while you wait?"

"The key to the soddy is on the ring with the truck key," she answered. "It's home to me now. I'll tell Ken and Lon that I'm staying there."

"It gets awful lonely out on the prairie by yourself. If you want me to keep you company, I will."

"No, May. You've got things to do and friends to see back in New York. As for me, I've got a project in mind, which is going to keep me busy for weeks on end. Besides, with the money I left in my account, I'm going to have a generator installed so I can watch TV in the evenings. But first of all, I'll buy me a cellular phone to call you every night so you won't worry."

"I've been worried about you since the day I took over your care. That's not about to change." Tears filled the older woman's eyes. "Judd Coltrain is all kinds of a fool for not knowing he's married to an angel. I'd pray him out of your life if I didn't know how much you wanted him in it."

"I do," Xan whispered urgently, hugging May hard before escorting her inside the terminal for a tearful goodbye. "No matter how badly things have started off, I refuse to give up on my marriage."

* * *

But when three weeks had gone by with no word from his brothers that Judd had returned from the cattle drive, doubts began to erode her initial optimism. She looked around the transformed soddy through blurry eyes, wondering if they would ever share it as man and wife.

During the long interim, Ken and Lon, who were overjoyed that she hadn't gone to New York, made constant visits to encourage her and help keep up her spirits. Each time they came, they brought her treats and magazines and tried to cheer her with stories about growing up in the Black Hills. She lived for their visits and couldn't help but be hungry for any information about Judd and his family.

It touched her heart that the soddy was the first home of their great-grandparents on Judd's father's side. Over the years, Judd had been the one to make the decision about keeping it and the surrounding land in mint condition for sentimental reasons. On occasional holidays, he allowed it to be opened to the public as a favor to the state of South Dakota. Apparently it was one of the best-preserved pioneer dwellings in the prairie states.

When Xan realized that the pile of quilting blocks she'd found in the old trunk had been made by Judd's great-grandmother, she considered it a labor of love to finish them and make the quilt as a special wedding present for him. In one corner, she added her own creation, a quilting block showing a dart poking into ground that represented the Bad River.

In her heart, she prayed that one day, years from now, a beloved great-granddaughter would point to that block with reverence and tell interested listeners the amazing and romantic story of how her own great-grandparents first met.

But as three weeks stretched into four, then five, and still no word, Xan's hopes began to shrivel. It appeared that Judd had no interest at all in the wife he'd left behind, no curiosity or desire to find out how she might be getting along.

Last night May had told her to give it up and come home, that no man was worth such a heavy price. This evening, as Xan drove the truck from Wall in the sweltering August heat, fighting the usual war with the grasshoppers, she decided that May was right. Waiting for something that was never going to happen made no sense at all.

When Xan saw one of the Lazy L Blazers parked in front of the soddy, she was relieved. Over the last five weeks she'd learned to love Judd's brothers and needed to say goodbye to them in person.

Jumping down from the cab, she hurried toward the house and opened the door. "I hope you haven't had to wai—"

But she never finished what she was going to say because it wasn't Lon or Ken who stood in the center of the soddy. This man was taller, broader shouldered, dressed in a navy shirt and light trousers, which molded his powerful thighs.

Xan's gaze traveled compulsively up the superb male physique to his hard, handsome face, now clean-shaven and darkly lean. No longer unruly, his thick black hair sprang from his scalp in a crisp wave.

His lancing green eyes rested on her features before they traveled over the rest of her, instantly striking up a strange tension that made her heart pound and her mouth go dry.

His arresting stance, combined with a commanding presence, put her in mind of a mysterious prince from a faraway kingdom, erasing forever the image of the dirt-poor farmer wearing a tattered T-shirt and ancient overalls.

Seeing him like this made her wonder at her temerity in imagining he would ever want to be her husband. She could easily believe that women made fools of themselves over him.

Undeniably, she'd been the biggest fool of all.

A man like Judd Coltrain didn't need to find a wife out of some newspaper. In his eyes she must be the most pathetic, demented and pitiful of all the designing females who had ever darkened his doorstep.

Embarrassment over what she'd done sent hot waves of color to her face and neck.

"I-if you're angry because I've been living here, rest assured that tomorrow morning I'll be gone." When he didn't say anything, she rattled on nervously. "I was in town making arrangements with a moving company to have everything that doesn't belong here put in storage so the place will be restored to its museumlike state."

Not daring to meet his eyes, she focused on the quilt he held grasped in his hands, the one that personified all her hopes and her tears.

"I—I hope you didn't mind that I put your great-grandmother's quilt together. The blocks were so beautiful I couldn't help myself."

Her words reverberated like an echo in the tiny room, increasing the tension.

"Why didn't you tell me you were Silas Harrington's granddaughter when we first met?" he asked in his deep voice, sounding even angrier than the morning he'd tossed her on the bed at the Lazy L.

It meant he'd received the papers from Mr. Raynor and knew everything.

In trepidation, she backed away from him. "Since I was taken to live with my grandfather, people have known that one day I'd inherit his company and his money. It's a situation I wouldn't wish on my worst enemy.

"Many men, including Todd Bramforth, a man my grandfather approved of and wanted me to marry, proposed to me more times than I can count, but I could never be sure if he or any of my oh-so-ardent and charming suitors were really in love with me. I'm not so different from you. According to Lon and Ken, you're the wealthiest rancher in South Dakota. Like you," she whispered, her gaze flashing to his face beseechingly, "I wanted to be loved for myself and no other reason."

Judd put the quilt on the bed, then stared at her once more, his dark head cocked, his brilliant eyes a slash of green through the black lashes.

"When you approached me at the booth, I took one look at you and believed you were the destitute rancher you purported to be. When you said it would take you ten more years to pay off your mortgage, I had no reason to think you were lying."

Swallowing hard, she admitted, "Y-you seemed a self-made man who wouldn't accept anyone's financial help, certainly not a woman's. Definitely not mine." Her voice quivered. "I admired you more than you can imagine for the fact that you worked by the sweat of your brow every day of your life and didn't expect help from any other source, not even your brothers.

"The men at the top who surrounded my grandfather were products of old money and Ivy League schools. They grew up with old-boy connections, a guaranteed entrée into moneyed society with all its attendant perks. I doubt that Todd or his kind have ever worked by the sweat of their brow, not one day in their entire lives.

"*You* were like a breath of fresh air," she confessed quietly. "A man who makes his own fires, who doesn't complain or find excuses, yet projects a sense of worth and dignity."

She bit her lip. "To be honest, I was charmed by you, by your old-fashioned ways. It touched and humbled me that on the advice of your brothers, you would drive all the way from your ranch to visit me at the booth. When you said you'd meet me at Pastor Swan's, I was convinced you were a God-fearing man who was worth knowing.

"At that point, the last thing I wanted to do was scare you away by telling you up front that I had more money than most people can imagine. I was

afraid you would think me shallow and unde-
serving. With hindsight, I can see that I should have
told you the truth, but you probably wouldn't have
believed me.''

She heard a harsh intake of breath. "You're
right. That night I wouldn't have believed one word
that came out of that exquisite lying mouth of
yours.''

His words sent a chill through her body, yet oddly
enough, her skin burned.

"Are you saying that you believe me now?''

He shifted his weight. "I've just returned from
New York. After being closeted with your attorney
for the greater part of a day, I spent the evening
with May at your grandfather's mansion. While she
fixed me dinner, I wandered into your grandfather's study and saw the map where the dart you
threw was still stuck in the Bad River.''

Xan blinked in astonishment.

"When I left, I took it with me for a souvenir.''

"You did?'' With her heart pounding in her
throat, her question came out more like a croak.

"Your story about the way you happened to pick
South Dakota to find yourself a husband was so
ludicrous, I decided it was possible you hadn't made
it up. When the opportunity arose, I looked for the
evidence to confirm my suspicions.''

"I see.'' She moistened her lips nervously.

He muttered an epithet that made her blush.
"What kind of monster was your grandfather to
leave you so vulnerable you'd prefer to throw
yourself and your fortune at a total stranger?''

She fought the tears that suddenly stung her eyes. "He wasn't a monster, Judd. Only a man driven by grief after my grandmother died. Some men love a woman that much. I suppose in my naive way, I was hoping to find a man who would love me as all-consumingly."

"And you thought *I* was that man?"

Struggling for poise, she said, "Yes. But I realize now, a love like that doesn't come along very often in life. I was a fool to think it did." Her voice cracked. "And I don't expect it to ever happen to me. If you don't want my grandfather's fortune, then set it up as a foundation to help the homeless or something. I want no more part of it. The mansion is May's until she dies, along with the investment that supports her. As for me, I'm going to get myself a new life."

Running a restless hand through her dark curls, she said, "If you've brought divorce papers with you, I'll sign them. However, if you prefer our marriage to exist on paper, as a ploy to keep fortune-hunting women at bay, that's fine with me, too. Either way, I'm leaving in the morning.

"Should you ever need my signature on anything, Mr. Raynor will always know where to get in touch with me. I think that's everything," she said in as bright a voice as she could muster considering her heart was breaking all over again. "So if you don't mind, I'd like to be left alone to get things ready and pack."

"Actually I do mind," he answered with unexpected force, causing her body to stiffen. "I promised to show you a jackalope and thought this evening might be as good a time as any."

Heat enveloped her face and body with alarming swiftness when she realized how gullible she'd been around Judd. She was so crazy about him, he could have told her anything and she would have believed him. The truth was, a jackalope was South Dakota's biggest joke on tourists. The locals took the head of a rabbit, attached antlers to it, then mounted it on a wall so that everyone who saw it would believe such an animal existed.

"Since you left, I've met up with dozens of them on every store wall in Wall, so it won't be necessary. Now if that's everything—"

"It's not!"

Her head flew back in surprise and their gazes collided. His eyes seemed to pierce her very soul.

"What happened to the woman who told me she loved me, who warned me I'd better show up at the wedding or she'd come find me on my ranch and live with me until the end of our days?"

Taking a fortifying breath, Xan said, "That woman was out of her mind, full of fantasies she created that had no part of reality."

"What happened to the woman who ate buffalo meat every day and night and said she loved it?" His voice rasped.

"That woman would have eaten dirt for the man she loved. But that woman no longer exists."

"No? Then what are you doing at the soddy when I expected to find you at home in New York?"

Hadn't his brothers told him anything?

"Because that's May's home now and I needed some privacy while I worked through my plans for the future."

"There are a lot of places you could have gone to be private. But you chose to remain here. Why?" he demanded, the tension so heavy the cords stood out in his neck.

"Because I like being incognito and I like the isolation," she blurted, totally out of sorts from his interrogation.

His eyes made a thorough scan of the interior, then flicked to hers. "I approve of the changes. It feels like a home should feel."

"Oh, stop it, Judd! You're not the charismatic, humble down-and-out rancher I thought you were, the one person who could call me ma'am and make it sound like an endearment. I'm sick of the lies."

"So am I," he ground out. "That's why I want the truth from you, and I want it now!"

"What truth?"

"That you've been waiting for me here, all this time, because you love me. You told me you loved me on our wedding day, remember?"

His goading tore her apart. Averting her eyes she said, "We were different people then."

His face drained of color. "So it was a lie after all, is that what you're saying?"

"No! Everything I said came straight from my heart," she admitted at long last. "But you trampled all over that love."

"Because I wanted to believe it too damn much."

Dear God. What was he saying?

The next thing she knew his hands grasped her shoulders and he forced her to look at him. But his countenance had changed. With a grim expression he said, "You could have no conception of the rage I was in the night I arrived at the rodeo grounds. Convinced that you and my brothers had set this whole thing up, I was ready to strangle you, sight unseen." Xan felt his hands tighten painfully, though she was certain he wasn't aware of it.

"But one look at you and a much more destructive emotion came to mind." His chest heaved. "Part of me wanted to expose you on the spot for the fraud you were. Another part—" he paused as if the words had to be dragged out of him "—wanted, *needed* to delay the day of reckoning."

She shook her head in bewilderment. "Why were you so ready to condemn me out of hand, Judd? Your brothers told me there was a time when they tried to do a little matchmaking. But surely their meddling, which was done out of love, couldn't possibly have upset you to *this* degree."

His jaw hardened before he said, "No." Then he let go of her and raked bronzed hands through his hair, as if his thoughts were too dark and heavy to tolerate. Xan stood with her arms pressed to her waist, waiting until he was ready to talk.

"There was a time when my brothers and I rode in the local rodeos. About five years ago, one of the queens of the rodeo, who was acquainted with our family and was an excellent rider, let me know she was interested in Lonnie and wanted my help in getting them together. Since I knew Lonnie was attracted, but didn't know how to break the ice, I agreed to help out.''

A long silence ensued while Xan tried to read between the lines. Judd's face hardened into an expressionless mask.

"Go on," she pressed urgently.

"Things went so well, Lonnie wanted to marry her and asked me if I'd loan him the money to buy her a ring because all his money was tied up with the ranch.

"Naturally I agreed, and he left right away for Rapid City, but his timing was off because it was in the middle of winter and a blizzard made it impossible for him to get back until late the next day. Since the ring was to have been a surprise, he didn't tell Katie where he was going. She came by the ranch unexpectedly and was disappointed when he wasn't there. Because of the storm, she was forced to stay overnight.''

By this time Xan had an idea what was coming and felt sick inside.

"About midnight, I had a visitor in my bedroom." At that confession, Xan moaned. "I learned just enough to realize that the only Coltrain who mattered to her was the one with the purse strings. As soon as she told the truth, all hell broke loose.''

No one knew what that experience could be like better than Xan, who shuddered at the pictures filling her mind. She almost had it in her heart to feel sorry for the foolish woman who been caught out by Judd.

"From that point on, I made certain she disappeared from our lives for good, but not until she'd broken it off with Lonnie in a way that didn't destroy his ego. Miraculously, Jenny appeared in his life soon after that. The rest is history."

At last everything made sense.

"So he never knew," she murmured.

"No. Part of the reason being that it was my fault for not seeing through her ploy in the first place."

She put a gentle hand on his arm. "Don't you mean the *whole* reason? For years you've tried to be both mother and father to your brothers, and when something went wrong that was out of your control, you took on that complete burden and have never forgiven yourself.

"No wonder you've been unable to trust women. She betrayed both of you, but Judd, not all women are like her." Xan's voice wobbled.

His head jerked around and he stared at her. "Don't you think I know that? Do you have any idea how much I love you? How much hell I've been going through since I left New York, racing to get back to you and beg your forgiveness, only to find that you'd disappeared off the face of the earth and I couldn't find you?"

"But your brothers *knew* where I was. So did May!" she cried breathlessly, so overjoyed by his admission that she was afraid she was dreaming.

"None of them said a word." His voice sounded ragged.

Swallowing hard, she whispered, "T-then how did you know I was here?"

"I didn't."

"But—"

"You *know* why I came here," he murmured emotionally. "Because this is the place where the magic happened to both of us, where our world was colored for all time."

A deep, husky timbre crept into his voice. His whole body trembled with the strength of his feelings, and she realized he was opening up his soul to her.

"I didn't know a love like yours was possible. You've transformed me. Give me one more chance and I'll prove to you that I'm the Bad man you've been looking for, that I'll be every one of those things you wanted. I swear it."

Trying to suppress her euphoria she said, "Do you swear you won't let the fortune I gave you be an issue between us?"

"Thank God for that fortune," he replied with stunning intensity. "Thank God for *this*."

He pulled the dart out of his shirt pocket.

She couldn't prevent the impish smile that crept over her face, and turned away from him so he couldn't see it. "Do you swear that you won't stab me with it one night in a sudden rage?"

"I swear I'll never be in another rage, not when I have a woman like you loving me."

"Careful, Mr. Coltrain. Don't make promises you can't keep."

"You're right. Just to be safe, I'll have it framed."

"That might be the best idea. Do you swear to take me to the Badlands on our honeymoon?"

"Xan—"

"Do you swear to take me now?"

When he didn't answer she said, "Do you swear that we can start our family tonight?"

She could tell he'd come to stand directly behind her. His body heat reached out to embrace her before strong arms reached around and almost crushed the air from her body.

"Mr. Coltrain?" she cried out, trying to catch her breath. "Did you hear anything I said?"

For an answer, she felt him bury his face against her neck. "Yes, ma'am," he drawled in thick tones she felt to the tips of her toes. "I heard it all. But I kind of had a hankering to take you out to the Bad River first. We've got unfinished business to attend to."

She let out a little moan of delight. "We do—"

For an answer, he held her tighter. "But you need to swear a couple of things to me first."

"Anything." She gasped the word.

"Swear that you'll never serve us buffalo meat again."

Xan started to laugh. She couldn't help it.

"Swear it," he insisted, kissing her cheek, her ear, her hair.

Finally she blurted, "I promise, as long as you promise to never wear overalls again."

"Done! Now swear that you'll do whatever I ask you to do next."

Her heart started to run away with her. "What do you mean, *whatever*?"

"Just swear it," he demanded in the authoritative tone she loved so much.

"Will I like it?"

"You'll never know until you swear it."

"Judd?" She was starting to get panicky. When she heard a wicked little chuckle deep in his throat, she felt slightly feverish.

"Yes, ma'am?"

"S-swear to love me forever?" Her voice caught.

"I already did that before God."

"But you thought I was a liar."

"That's right."

"And you married me anyway?"

"Couldn't help myself. You bewitched me the first night I laid eyes on you. I've been doomed ever since. Now, if there aren't any more questions, swear you'll start filling that tub over in the corner for this exhausted rancher whose finally home and wants a little peace and comfort with his wife."

"Mr. Coltrain!"

"Why, Mrs. Coltrain. How you *do* blush. Don't you know this is what nice little girls get for throwing caution to the wind and advertising for a *Bad* man?"

BRIDE'S BAY RESORT

UNLOCK THE DOOR TO GREAT ROMANCE AT BRIDE'S BAY RESORT

Join Harlequin's new across-the-lines series, set in an exclusive hotel on an island off the coast of South Carolina.

Seven of your favorite authors will bring you exciting stories about fascinating heroes and heroines discovering love at Bride's Bay Resort.

Look for these fabulous stories coming to a store near you beginning in January 1996.

Harlequin American Romance #613 in January
Matchmaking Baby by Cathy Gillen Thacker

Harlequin Presents #1794 in February
Indiscretions by Robyn Donald

Harlequin Intrigue #362 in March
Love and Lies by Dawn Stewardson

Harlequin Romance #3404 in April
Make Believe Engagement by Day Leclaire

Harlequin Temptation #588 in May
Stranger in the Night by Roseanne Williams

Harlequin Superromance #695 in June
Married to a Stranger by Connie Bennett

Harlequin Historicals #324 in July
Dulcie's Gift by Ruth Langan

Visit Bride's Bay Resort each month wherever Harlequin books are sold.

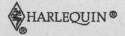

HARLEQUIN ®

Bestselling authors

ELAINE
COFFMAN
RUTH LANGAN

and

MARY McBRIDE

Together in one fabulous collection!

Available in June wherever Harlequin
books are sold.

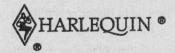

HARLEQUIN ®

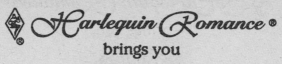

Harlequin Romance ®

brings you

How the West Was Wooed!

We've rounded up twelve of our most popular authors, and the result is a whole year of romance, Western style. Every month we'll be bringing you a spirited, independent woman whose heart is about to be lassoed by a rugged, handsome, one-hundred-percent cowboy! Watch for...

HITCH-5

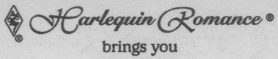
Harlequin Romance ®

brings you

HERO
HOLDING OUT FOR A

Some men are worth waiting for!

They're handsome, they're charming but, best of all,
they're single! Twelve lucky women are about to
discover that finding Mr. Right is not a problem—it's
holding on to him.

In June the series continues with:

#3411 THE DADDY TRAP
by Leigh Michaels

Hold out for Harlequin Romance's heroes in
coming months...

♦ July: **THE BACHELOR'S WEDDING**—Betty Neels

♦ August: **KIT AND THE COWBOY**—Rebecca Winters

♦ September: **REBEL IN DISGUISE**—Lucy Gordon

HOFH-6